RIOT RADIO
JADE STONE
AF253331

Riot Radio
Copyright © 2018 by Jade Stone

Tellwell Talent
www.tellwell.ca

ISBN
978-0-2288-0391-1 (Hardcover)
978-0-2288-0390-4 (Paperback)
978-0-2288-0392-8 (eBook)

RIOT RADIO

BY JADE STONE

ACKNOWLEDGEMENTS

I would like to thank my mother and father for always believing in me. Since I was a young girl, I have wanted to be writer and they have supported me through this entire journey. I would like to thank my close friends who have read my works and have such enthusiasm for my dream. And to my cats for keeping me company while I spend hours on the computer.

Chapter 1

WELCOME TO RIOT RADIO, WEIRDOS

"**HELLO** everyone!" My voice crackles over the airwaves. "Welcome to Riot Radio! Kick out the jams, motherfuckers!" I press 'play' and *I Wanna Be Your Dog* by Iggy Pop and the Stooges blasts over the airwaves.

I might as well introduce myself. I'm Sasha, a punk rock girl, a freak among freaks. Even other freaks look at me like I don't belong. Leather jacket, leather skirt, fishnets, black and red dyed hair. You probably think what I'm saying is shit, that I look like any other punk. But I'm awkward as fuck. I blend into the background, taking everything in; I watch your every move until I know what you're really like; and, I'm only confident talking over the air.

Full disclosure depression, anxiety and addiction have been following me my whole life. Trying not to relapse is a constant fucking battle that I haven't won yet. But I will never fucking give up. Punks don't give up. Fact according to Sasha.

You are probably wondering how a girl like me got her own fucking radio station. This old guy used to own this place when it was a record store. I'd go there all the time and since he had no family, he left it to me. Now I got my own space and a kick-ass inventory to boot.

When the Iggy Pop track ends, I put on *Oh Woe is Me* by Joan Jett and the Blackhearts, one of her signature, nasty tracks. I light a cigarette and lean back on my black velvet couch. I close my eyes, letting the smoke fill my lungs.

Let me take you back to how it all began. It was high school in the 2010s and I was a freak there too, the quiet kind. I wasn't a punk rock wallflower then—just your ordinary fucking wallflower. I didn't really talk much, but that really didn't matter because everyone was as boring as hell and I didn't want to talk to them anyway. But I listened, and I didn't miss a fucking thing.

Vinyl was starting to explode … again. It was 2010 and kids my age wanted vinyl records and they wanted the fucking Beatles. I saw Beatles posters everywhere: kids were on Tumblr posting Beatle pics, Beatle gifs and McLennon shit. McLennon is the name people gave what they hoped was a relationship (a 'ship') between John Lennon and Paul McCartney—you know, a *real* relationship, if you get my drift.

> Then there was me—sitting in my fucking freezing basement in my vintage, white-lace top and brown, leather mini-skirt, my long, light-brown hair trailing down my back, huge retro headphones on my head, eyes closed, listening to Girl from the Rubber Soul album:
>
> Is there anybody going to listen to my story
> All about the girl who came to stay?
>
> I would spend hours listening to that shit, John Lennon's nasally voice filling my ears, me holding

the album cover, writing thoughts, lyrics, poems in a brown leather notebook.

Flash to the city: me with my hippy outfit and flower choker, walking the streets like I own them. It's different from walking the halls at school where I walked with my head down and my hands tight around my backpack.

Today is the day I walk into Criminal Records. The shop is pretty cool. It has racks lined with band shirts and vinyls are spread out in the middle of the room.

"Hey let me know if you could use some help," someone says. I look up and see a guy behind the counter. His white hair is in a ponytail down to his hips. He is wearing a white shirt with a suede vest that looks it came from the 60s and John Lennon glasses. It is like seeing a fucking rock star— someone who was actually there when the good music happened.

For a moment I stand like an idiot trying to get words out. "I … I really like the Beatles but I already have all their albums. Would you recommend anything?"

He smiled wide. "Led Zeppelin."

CHAPTER 2

WHO THE FUCK IS LED ZEPPELIN?

He went through the vinyl. "Start with Zeppelin Four, Black Dog," he says. I nod like he just imparted scared wisdom: I buy the record.

Led Zeppelin is the heavy metal of the 60s: Robert Plant, the lead singer, has a voice range that goes high to low, no middle ground. But that didn't matter. Jimmy Page's searing guitar and John Bonham's heavy drumming do more than fill the fucking gaps. Almost immediately, I ditch the flower crown and suede skirt for vintage jeans up to my waist and a white Led Zeppelin crop top. I curl my hair to look like Robert Plant and Jimmy Page.

A few days later I saunter back into Criminal records and sit on the counter. Rick—with his long, majestic white ponytail—grins. "How's my young hippy friend?" he asks.

"Better, now that I'm here." Led Zeppelin's Houses of the Holy is playing on the record player. Softer stuff but it still kicks ass.

"It's been slow today … want to smoke up?" I freeze. I never did a drug in my fucking life, but I nod anyway. You can't be a fucking hippy if you don't smoke pot.

"Lets' go," Rick says. I follow him to the back and he takes out a green bong and lights up. He takes a deep breath and sighs. "Your turn."

I take it, trying to not let my hands shake. I'm nervous. What if I go on a bad trip and go around the city chasing what I think are evil garden gnomes or go into a fucking drug coma? I take a deep breath and let the smoke fill my lungs. For a moment there's nothing—then everything calms down and a lazy smile crosses my lips. The anxiety is gone. Every fearful thought is gone and I feel hazy and calm.

Then I start to giggle like an idiot. "Can you fucking believe Ode to Joy kicked out Robert Plant?"

"The fuck!"

"Ode to Joy is the first band that Robert Plant was in. He was kicked out because his band mates thought he couldn't sing ! Can you fucking believe it? "

"I hear ya, man." He leans back, eyes closed.

Later, that day high school me that just did drugs for the first time goes home. I stare at the fire I have just made … in which I am burning all my hippy shit. My eyes are wide; I am still high as fuck.

There is a knock at the door of Riot Radio that pulls me away from thinking of my recent hippy past and how I burned it all in one night and I get up to open the door. There's Jamie leaning on the door frame, his brown eyes flashing and his brown hair falling into them. There's always been this darkness in Jamie's eyes, something I have tried to ignore since I met him.

My eyes follow the tattoos up and down his arms as he asks with a twisted grin, "Ready to rejoin the world?"

"Do I have to?" I say, my face twisting in annoyance. I put out my cigarette on the concrete floor of Riot Radio grinding it dead with my black, leather, knee-high boots. "We could just stay here and not deal with anyone's shit."

"Well, there is no food—or WiFi for that matter," Jamie says with his signature twisted grin.

"We don't need WiFi to survive," I protest.

"This from the girl who obsessively checks Instagram," he says, laughing bitterly.

"Hey, how else can I stalk Joan Jett and Billie Joe Armstrong at the same time?"

"You do realize he killed punk rock, right?" he says, lifting one perfectly-shaped eyebrow.

"Shut the fuck up, Jamie. He sang about emotion. Is that a fucking crime?" I demand.

"If it's punk then yes, it's a fucking crime."

"He's fucking hot. You have to admit it." I say.

"Okay, I'll give you that. He's hot as fuck," he says, purring. Jamie is gay as fuck. I'm gay as fuck. There you go. I just came out.

Jamie talked me into going out to eat.

"You don't have to walk me home," I protest after we've eaten. Dark streets with sketchy-ass people don't scare me.

"Yes, I do. It's one in the morning."

"I thought you were a feminist?" I say, raising an eyebrow.

"I am a feminist ... but you are so *little*," he says, pretending to pat my head.

"I bite," I tell him.

"I know you do," he says letting his bitter Jamie laugh out for my benefit.

"How's what's-his-face, the guy you're dating?" I ask.

"Fuck me." He sighs. I watch him bury his face in his hands. "I came home and he was fucking this blonde guy on my bed. I was burning his shit all day."

"Asshole!" I sneer. "Want me to cuss him out on Riot Radio? Maybe a bunch of punks will go kick his ass."

"Tempting," Jamie says, hands covering his face again.

"I can sneak attack him myself," I offer.

"Also tempting." He squeezes my hand tight. That's Jamie saying 'I need you' without words.

Chapter 3

MY NEW GAY NEIGHBOUR ... I'M GAY TOO, I'M JUST EXCITED, DON'T JUDGE ME

I'M doing a rare thing and venturing out of my apartment. If I don't check the mail, a giant pile starts to grow and that just brings more fucking anxiety, not something I need.

I spot someone I have never seen before in the hall—head down, curly black hair and heading towards me.

"Hey, neighbour!" I say, way too fucking cheerfully as I take in his deep, blue eyes.

"Oh, um, hi," he mumbles.

Normally I wouldn't go near my neighbours because they might actually want to talk to me. But he looks cute ... so I'm creeping him for Jamie. I saunter over before I lose the balls to do so.

"Are you, or have you ever been an asshole?" I ask.

"Um … I don't think so." His deep, blue eyes dance nervously. "Are you the undercover asshole police?" he says, giving me a shaky smile.

"Yes, you have found me out," I laugh. "I'm creeping you for a friend."

"Oh, okay … that's a little less weird, I guess." He laughs nervously again. "I'm gay though," he says softly, almost like an apology.

"Good so is he. Want his number?"

"Um, okay."

Sweet! This could have gone sideways and he could have called the cops to report, 'There's a strange girl outside trying to set me up and I think her sanity is questionable'.

"You got a pen and paper?" I ask. "I kind of came out here unprepared."

"Uh, I've got my phone." He hands me his phone and I enter Jamie's number.

"Okay, um cool," he says.

"Cool. I gotta go be weird in my apartment now."

"Ok. Bye," he says looking amused but really fucking confused all at the same time.

I'm lying down on my red and black velvet sheets listening to the female lead of *Vice Squad* scream in my ear about the destruction of London. She's walking through the rubble singing the saddest punk song I ever fucking heard. It sends shivers down my bare arms.

I lay back thinking about punk bands becoming fucking mainstream. They formed to shake up the fucking world, to spit in the face of the fucking establishment. If everyone knows them—like the Clash, like the fucking Sex Pistols—they become the opposite of what punk is about.

It's fucking ironic, punk is supposed to be an outlet for the fucking freaks … but when a bunch of people hear punk bands and think they' re cool because they follow them then they become mainstream.

I close my eyes trying not to think about how the masses are taking away my sanity. There's a knock at my door and I bolt upright. No one ever knocks. Maybe it's the new neighbour kid wanting to talk about Jamie.

I rush to the door and I fucking freeze as I slowly open the door. There is a girl at the door. Her wide grey eyes stare at me through the thick black eyeliner around them. My heart is hammering too hard in my chest. I anxiously clutch at my dirty tank top. I open the door a bit more. *Psycho Killer* by the Talking Heads pulses inside my skull.

> *Psycho Killer – Qu'est-ce que c'est*
> *Fa-fa-fa-fa-fa-fa-fa-fa-fa-far better*
> *Run, run, run, run, run, run, run, away oh oh oh*

I let out a breath when I see the girl behind the door doesn't have an axe or whatever weapon psycho killers favour these days. I take her in through narrowed eyes. She has long, twisting brown hair with curls of silver.

I open the door and her grey, painted eyes scan my room, taking in the mess of vinyl, CDS, and falling posters. She is all blue. Blue velvet tank and tight turquoise leather skirt; blue fishnets decorate her legs and a blue leather jacket drapes over her body. She has a guitar strapped to her back. The red heart grenade from the cover of Green Day's *American Idiot* pulses in my head, threatening to explode. I see a bleeding image of her holding a grenade in one hand, a cigarette in another.

"I like your place," she says with a French accent. "The fucking super isn't here yet with my key so I thought I'd say hello. She seems to have a confidence that I can only fake. While my confidence can be torn down way too easily, she is exuding one that seems to be fucking bulletproof.

"I'm Sophia."

"Sasha."

"I love it! Our names are so similar!"

"What do you do Sasha?"

"I run a radio station."

"Amazing! I love America! "I've come to be in a band. I'm very excited. You should come over sometime!"

Who is this girl who walks into my fucking apartment like she's known me her whole life and then invites me over like we are old friends? Who does that?"

"Yeah … sounds good." I say planning never to see her again.

"Okay, well I'm going to find the fucking super. Nice to meet you, Sasha."

"Uh ... same here."

She's hot, but she doesn't do anything for me. Sometimes I feel I just used my sex drive up completely and now the only thing that gets me going is my job and the foam on top of lattes.

CHAPTER 4

I GAVE A RANDOM GUY JAMIE'S NUMBER OR CH-CH-CH-CHERRY BOMB ... WHATEVER

JAMIE is walking with me to Riot Radio and I can't stop smiling.

"You smile like that when you're up to something … spill, girl," he says, examining the flawless black nail polish on his fingernails.

"There is this cute guy living beside me and he's gay! I gave him your number."

Jamie narrows his eyes and lets out a sigh that is reserved for the everyday annoyances of life. "You do know that we won't just automatically like each other just because we're both gay, right?" he says through narrowed, black-painted eyes.

"He's fucking cute. You should be thanking me."

"Yes, thank you for giving some random creep my number," he says, rolling his eyes with a condescension he has perfected over the years.

"You *will* be thanking me."

Jamie just rolls his eyes. "Of course I will, girl."

"Here's your stop," he says as we get to the record store. "See you in the morning, little sprite."

I step into Riot Radio and make myself a cup of coffee to wake up my brain. I pour in the cream and sugar and I start flipping through my records. The itch that comes when I go through my records grows as I search for the first record of the day. It's fucking crucial to pick a good one. If people turn you off in the first few minutes, they aren't fucking coming back.

I pull out the Runaways' first record. Only Cherie Currie, the lead singer, is on the cover. If I was in the band I'd be fucking pissed. Your first exposure in the music world and you're not even on the fucking cover! I place the album on the record player. Cherie Currie snarls,

> *Can't stay at home, can't stay at school,*
> *Old folks say, 'You poor little fool'*

As it rips through the speakers, it brings me back to when I first heard of the Runaways.

I'm sixteen years old in my third year of high school and I'm sitting in the basement of my parents house on a threadbare, plaid couch with my waist high jeans and white Led Zeppelin crop top on. I've just put on the Runaways movie. There is a picture of two badass girls on the cover, so why the fuck not watch it when I have nothing better to do. Images flash on the tiny ancient TV. Two young girls with golden blonde hair rebelling by using a mirror to put on makeup in a dirty and sketchy gas station bathroom. A girl with choppy black hair and a 'dare you to fuck with me' look on her face is buying a guy's black leather jacket. She's running down the street with it on like her life depended on it. A song called Wild One is playing. "All my life I wanted to be someone and here I am!" screams Suzi Quatro, the lead singer, without giving a fuck about how she sounds. "I know what I got and there ain't nobody / gonna take it away from me/ so let me tell you what I am."

There is this feeling that is going underneath my skin. I want that to be me. I want to cut my hair off. I want to fight the next asshole who looks at me. I want that 'I dare you to fuck with me' look. I want a black leather jacket. I want to be Joan-fucking-Jett.

After the movie, I jump up and take the next train into the city. This urge, this fucking hunger underneath my skin eats at me the whole ride down. I can barely sit still, my legs shake up and down and people stare at me on the train.

I walk into Kops Records. It's a tight record store that has a lot of indie and classic rock records. The punk section has a Sex Pistols poster behind it—the Union Jack with a picture of the queen gagged and blinded by the words 'God Save The Queen'. I stalk down the aisles of the classic rock section, go to the 'R' section and I see them on the cover an album: the fucking Runaways. Girls playing rock and roll. Girls my age playing rock and roll.

I flip the record around eagerly. My favourite songs, Cherry Bomb and You Drive Me Wild are listed on the back cover. I don't even look at the price. It's my fucking record now. That hunger is growing. I want all their records. I want everything the fucking Runaways ever made. I go to pay for it, watching the cashier through eyes thickly lined with black eyeliner.

"Hey, you like the Runaways?" I look up to see a guy smiling at me, blinding me with his white fucking teeth. He's young, but not as young as me. That saying in the hippy world, 'Don't trust anyone over thirty' ... Well he's pushing thirty and I'm not sure about him. He's wearing a flawless black, leather jacket and has silver skull rings decorating his fingers.

"That movie was cool," he says. "We got Live in Japan behind me ... you want it?" I look up to see all the girls on the cover this time, three of them holding guitars.

"I'll fucking take it."

CHAPTER 5

SASHA BUYS A LEATHER JACKET ... FINALLY, WHAT THE FUCK TOOK YOU SO LONG?

I go to the Black Market, the most notorious vintage market in the city. I need a leather jacket, just like in the Runaways movie and this is the place to get it. I walk down the stairs into the market. The walls of the stairwell are painted white and black; it feels like I'm going down a black hole.

Downstairs, there are racks and racks of clothes jammed together. Black band tees with distorted images line the wall. There's a small record store called Short Stack Records in the back that sells obscure Pink Floyd and Rolling Stones shit. Beside it is a barber shop where people with tattoos lounge in chairs, getting their hair shaved. I roam through the store. I see feminist patches, dirty old spiked leather bracelets, rows of kick-ass vintage shoes with leather and camouflage on them. I stop at where the signs say 'jackets'. I push through thick old leather. I stop when I see black—and there it is. I lift it up and take it in. It's simple. There's no anarchy, like the spikes and studs of a punk jacket. The only studs are on the pop-out collar; otherwise the leather is soft and it ends at my hips. Just like in the movie. The hunger spikes; this jacket doesn't just feed it, it makes it grow. It's fucking perfect.

I pull down the Led Zeppelin crop top in annoyance. If I keep the top I'll just look like a hardcore Led Zeppelin fan. I go over to the T-shirts, guarding the leather jacket under my arm. I go through the tanks and tees until I find a white tank with The Sex Pistols written on it. It says Sex Pistols in black like someone wrote it in black permanent marker. It's torn through with holes. It's perfect.

I weave through the racks of clothes and find the change rooms in the back of the store. I go in. Only a red velvet curtain separates me from the world. Anxiety knots in my stomach; I take my keys in my knuckles just in case. I slip off the crop top and put on the tank and then the leather jacket. I close my eyes feeling the soft leather on my skin. It gives me a charge, causing my hairs to stand on end. I pause. Just another girl rebelling against nothing. Just a girl with this feeling ... this desperate feeling to be a wild one. Just like Joan Jett when she bought her first leather jacket.

I gather my courage. I'm ready to see myself. I reach for the velvet curtain then stop, holding a handful of velvet. I can do this. I will myself to step out and turn around. I open my eyes and freeze. I look in the mirror and ... I look like a wild one. I feel right.

At home, I listen to song after song by the Runaways, frantically looking up the lyrics on my phone as I immerse myself into googling them. I love them, with their fuck-you attitudes and their badass vintage clothes. Nothing eased the hunger to emulate them; it grew to spread into every inch of me.

It grew to the point where I would spend hours downtown, going through dusty vinyl in record shops owned by aging punks. I go to used book stores and ask the owners for books on the Runaways. A lot of them stared at me like I'm a just a young girl who has no idea what she is fucking talking about.

The other ten percent give me a slow smile. They know exactly what I want.

CHAPTER 6

DEPRESSION AND LOOKING LIKE SUZI QUATRO

I'M up late as usual at Riot Radio fighting to stay awake. The coffee just isn't cutting it anymore. I'm playing *Wild One* by Ms. Suzi Quatro and I can feel my eyes getting heavy. I'm going to rest them just for a minute between songs.

I'm looking at myself in my gold mirror. With my mess of dirty blonde hair, I look like Suzi Quatro, the girl who inspired Joan Jett to pick up a guitar. I want to look like Joan fucking Jett.

I go to the bathroom and cover my head in black hair dye, letting Love is Pain by Joan Jett fill the room. My thoughts go to the scene in the Runaways when the fucking band falls apart and Joan is self-harming in the bathtub screaming the lyrics to Love is Pain, her choppy black hair sticking to her pale skin, her eyes stained with faded black eyeliner, soaking in dirty bath water.

I soak my head under the water in the sink and wonder for a moment what it would be like to stay there. Just disappear forever in the water. Let the sadness take me. It pulls at my thoughts, like a siren urging me to drown in the waves. Water pushes against my lungs and panic erupts in my brain, screaming at me not do this. I come out from under the water, tears streaming down my face. I sink to the piercing, cold tile floor, pulling my knees to my chest. The sadness almost won. It almost won.

I wake up and realize the album is finished. It feels like my lungs are full of that water. My chest is heaving, hard. I need something to chase the memory away. I rush to the go on the air.

"You just heard the first side of the Runaways first record," I tell my listeners "If it didn't change your life, go get your head examined."

I put on *Rebel, Rebel* by Bowie. I reach for the familiar bottle of vodka. I take a swig, letting it run hot down my throat. I close my eyes and I'm back under the water, trying to end my life at fucking sixteen years old. I put the bottle back down. I light a joint instead. The smoke fills my lungs and a haze grows in my brain. I get high until I'm not sure that memory of trying to drown myself really happened.

CHAPTER 7

FIRST LOVE AND OTHER PAINFUL SHIT

I am at Riot Radio playing *I'll Come Crashing* by A Giant Dog, my eyes squeezed tight shut.

There's nothing in my nature that tells me not to do bad things …

The lyrics sear through my brain, an explosion of black and purple bleeds through my thoughts. A girl playing electric guitar, sneering into a mic. It brings me back to the comforting feeling of the leather jacket on my skin and me grinning, thinking I'm some sort of badass.

The high of the weed buzzes behind my shut eyes. I fade into a memory of a tiny speaker in the corner of the room playing *Lucy in the Sky with Diamonds* by the Beatles.

John Lennon's nasally voice telling us to picture ourselves in a boat on a river with orange trees and marmalade skies. The images bleed orange and yellow, carrying me down the river. Its like I'm there and I'm floating ever so slowly to paradise. I bring myself back only to see her, Melanie. My first crush. We are in her room high as fuck and listening to the Beatles. Perfect. Her blonde hair is spread across the pillow. She's wearing a black leather jacket and a slow smile is creeping across her face. I lean down ever so slowly, my lips just daring to brush hers. Her tongue is braver than mine, it 's exploring my mouth. I'm taking her leather jacket off slowly. Then everything goes to hell.

The door bursts open, slamming into the wall. The noise propels us away from each other—like I burned her. Her father's face is crimson red. His mouth twists in disgust. He's screaming, but I can't hear a word—adrenaline pulses too hard in my ears. Then I hear that word, that word I've heard whispered my whole life. I've never heard it screamed before.

Dyke! You fucking Dyke!

I wanted to scream at him that he can't call me that, that he knows nothing about me. I want my fist to collide with his face and hear his nose break. But I can't move. Fear is twisting inside me, tears are stinging my eyes from the fear and the shame. I just want to get out of this alive.

He grabs my hair and I try so hard not to scream. Pain explodes in my head, humiliation throughout my being. Don't hurt me—I want to say that, but nothing comes out. I feel my back collide with the wall. The pain travels from the back of my head all the way down my body. The tears come freely now. I gather all my anger and manage to stand up.

I swing at him, hard. The fucker's nose breaks and I grin over my small victory. He grabs me and his arms tighten around me, squeezing the air out of my lungs. I thrash violently to be free. I'm screaming with all the air I have left. Tears keep streaming down my face. Melanie just looks at me. She doesn't move. I'm thrown onto the road, the gravel stings my skin. I get up, all my limbs shaking. I'm sobbing now, the snot catching in my mouth. I can feel the blood drip down my knees as I limp home.

My body jolts as I awake from the memory. I open my eyes and hear a scream ripping from my throat. I grab things off the table, desperation searing through my veins. I throw them to the floor, glass shatters everywhere. I'm screaming, taking anything I can and throwing it to the floor. Anger pulsing; shame, humiliation. I want my fist to collide with his nose again; I want to hear bones break.

I take Riot Radio off the air and slam the door behind me. I march to my apartment, rage barely contained under my skin. The night air and the stars settle into my bones, making me become my anger, dark as the night. The empty hole in my chest sucks everything in. I open the door and hear it slam against the wall. I slump down against the door frame.

In my despair, I hear Sophia gently asking me if I'm okay.

As Sophia bends down towards me, I grab her shirt in my fist. She smiles in delight. As we head towards my bedroom I take off her shirt and my hand trails to her pants. I hastily unzip them, yank them off and throw her onto the bed. My nails dig into her skin. I'm in control. She's laughing at my aggro but her body responds to me. Groping hands and tongues … it's too much. It's over almost as soon as it begins and she leaves. I fall into a dark, angry sleep.

Bad memories and regret crawl under my skin, pulsing behind my eyes. I remember his bloated face twisted in disgust. Melanie's huge blue eyes watching me on my knees, I remember the fear when he grabbed my hair in his fist. My face hitting the gravel and me limping home, broken in two. I open my eyes. My blanket is over my head.

Broken girl, riot grrrl, queer girl, broken girl.

Groggily, I get up and make a cup of coffee. I step into the hallway to get my mail and see Ben.

"Oh hey, Sasha."

"Hey, Ben," I say not looking at him.

"Are you okay?" he asks.

I can't bear to look at his beautiful blue eyes. "More fucked up than usual," I mutter.

"Okay … I was going to ask if, um, Jamie is still single but we can talk about that another time."

I pause. "You got anything to drink in your apartment?"

I'm lying on Ben's dated pink-flowered couch as the last piece of the memory comes back to me, hazy and blurred.

I remember a warm buzz in my brain. I trip over my own feet, laughter escaping from my throat, the bottle almost slipping through my fingers. I stop when I see the white, painted house. I clutch my hand around the rock I'm carrying. It feels strong and powerful in my palm. My rage gathers, dark and insistent, like a black hole sucking in all my fear and the voices in my head that are telling me not to do this. Anger bubbles hot in my chest and I twist back my arm. I throw the rock at their living-room window. Glass shatters and I scream in victory. Melanie comes outside. Her father comes out too, with that same look of disgust on his face.

"You can't keep us apart, you homophobic piece of shit!" I scream, with spit coming out of my mouth. I shake harder with each word. "We're in love! Love, you fucking, fat asshole!" I scream, my face burning red. I hate the tears that come.

"Sasha, leave," she whispers. Then, she says something—something that shattered my world.

"You fucking coward! You are a fucking coward!" I scream.

The bottle is still in my hand. I'm about to say more when I hear sirens. I throw the bottle, watching it break against the wall of the house. Then I run, tears stinging, air ripping from my lungs. My chest aches like my heart is ready to explode. I run until my knees buckle in. I duck into a path and fall to the ground. I'm covered in dirt, makeup dripping into my eyes as it mixes and burns with my tears.

"Fuck you!" I sob as the words catch in my throat. My head spins. My hands grab at my hair and my body shakes. I cry until no more tears come. My head hangs and I'm unable to move.

As I shake, my world comes back into focus. Ben is bending over, looking for something to drink. I look at his mess of curly black hair and the loose-fitting band shirt he's wearing.

"I've got peach schnapps. Not really helping the gay stereotype," he says with nervous laughter escaping his lips.

"I'll take it."

He pours us some in red paper cups and sits next to me on the faded couch. I drink it down in one shot, pushing the memory down hard.

"So, what's Jamie like? Is he nice?" he asks, picking at his fingernails nervously.

I laugh. "Nice isn't something I'd use to describe Jamie."

I watch alarm grow on Ben's face. His deep blue eyes are wide and his pink lips are parted slightly.

"He's smart. And he's loyal. He's got tattoos and pretends to be a hardcore badass," I say taking in Ben's face as he looks at me intently.

"He's funny and he's gentle. He'll tell you he likes metal, but he loves pop-punk." I watch Ben begin to smile at the picture I'm painting of Jamie.

"He loves lattes with a bit of cinnamon. He will roll his eyes the whole time you take him to a Starbucks. He loves to read, but he only goes to used books stores."

"He sounds a bit like a pretentious hipster," Ben says, but he's smiling wistfully now, leaning back against the faded couch, his huge blue eyes focused on me.

"He's not, he's just a weirdo." I love the way the booze makes my head buzz, blurring everything. Then that voice. That fucking voice.

"Ben, I gotta go. Give Jamie a fucking call, 'k?" That surprised look overtakes Ben's face again.

"Yeah, yeah I will."

"Don't worry he doesn't bite." I rush out trying to ignore the confusion on Ben's face and the nagging feeling that maybe I hurt him. When I get back to my apartment, I lie on the floor, eyes wide, feeling almost numb except for that ache in my chest, listening to *Love is Pain*. Should be *life* is a pain. The room spins. I close my eyes, waiting for sleep to take me.

CHAPTER 8

JAMIE HAS A CRUSH ... JAMIE ACTUALLY HAS EMOTIONS? WHO KNEW?

JAMIE is grinning at me while we walk around Toronto's Queen Street East.

"What? Why are you staring at me like that?" I say pretending to be annoyed, but there is a laugh in my voice. There's always a laugh in my voice when it comes to Jamie.

"A guy called me saying that you gave him my number."

"Excuse me for trying to find someone who isn't a douche bag," I joke playfully. "Y'know, so you don't have to burn his stuff after." I poke his shoulder, laughing.

"You always have to burn their stuff," Jamie says, letting out a bitter sigh. Then, "He sounds cute. Is he cute?" he purrs.

"You know I can't tell. I'm gay as fuck."

But got to admit he's kind of pretty. I would never admit that to Jamie though.

Jamie sighs. "We're going for coffee tomorrow. Better be cute," he says, tilting his head at me.

"You're shallow, you know that?" I say, still with that laughter in my voice.

Jamie purrs, " I want them to have a good personality and not be fucking boring, but if I'm going to get to know them they have to be cute," he says, grinning at me.

"So fucking shallow," I say laughing.

"So, the girl you're fucking isn't hot?" I freeze and anxiety gathers tight in my chest.

"How the fuck did you know?" I whisper. I've stopped moving. I'm not like Jamie who brags about them. I don't like to talk about the people I fuck, not at all.

"You weren't at Riot Radio yesterday afternoon. So, it means you are either stuffing a burrito in your face or you're fucking." Jamie looks at me through narrow, painted eyes.

"Shit, I gave it away," I whisper to myself.

"Do I know her?"

"No, no one does," I mumble.

"Do I get to meet her? You met my potentially cute guy."

"That's not fucking fair, he's my neighbour."

"All is fair in war and hooking up," Jamie says as he purrs and winks.

CHAPTER 9

I'M A PUNK NOW

I'M at Riot Radio playing the Sex Pistols song *No Feelings*. I'm thinking back to how I become a stone-cold, pissed-off punk.

There I am, shutting off my feelings, shutting off the world. Staring into my gold mirror swearing to myself that I will never love anyone again, that I'll only be pissed and pissed off. I go to my closet and put on my spiked leather jacket, now embellished with punk patches. I'm going to the city to get fucked up.

Hours later and I'm at a club downtown. A punk band plays on the stage. The lead singer has a blonde spiked mohawk and is growling into the mic, slurring his words, like a blonde Sid Vicious. It's everything a punk bar should be: dingy, dark, and smelling like sweat, piss and beer.

I strut over to the bar in my torn, red jeans. My eyes wander over to a girl in a leather jacket. Long, brown hair falls into her face, almost covering her hazel eyes. I sit next to her and order a beer. The fucking bartender barely looks at the fake ID I got from a sleaze at school for a bunch of crumpled-up sweaty dollars.

I drink, letting the punk music fill my mind. Two beers later and I have a sweet buzzing in my brain. I lean in, "I like your jacket."

She smiles with her red, painted lips. "I like yours, too," she says, laughing.

"What are you drinking? I'll buy you one," I say.

"Gin and tonic," she says, smiling sweetly at me.

Before the drink comes she's leaning in, her lips brushing mine. In not much time at all we are alone in the bathroom. My back hits the coolness of the bathroom wall, but I don't care: her hands are under my shirt and her tongue is in my mouth. So much for looking sweet. Her hands trail down my legs. Fuck love, I'm just going to fuck.

Later, I go home, laughing and tripping over myself. It takes me a moment to notice my parents in the living room, silent with their eyes boring into me.

"What?" I ask, laughing.

"Are you drunk?" my mother demands, tears filling her eyes.

"What was your first fucking clue?" I shoot back, laughing, loving the pain I cause her.

"Don't talk to your mother like that!" my father snaps on cue. "Where were you?Who were you with?" he demands.

"I don't know, some random, fucking girl." I smile as their eyes widen. "I was fucking her! What you going to do about it?" I ask, grinning.

Later that night I'm dragging my bags down the street, sobered up, my hands shaking. They threatened this before, but I never thought they would go through it. My chest is tight, my anxiety overwhelming me. I get on the late bus and stare out the window, finally letting the tears fall. I play the Distillers for punk rock courage. I never went back.

CHAPTER 10

THE BEARD IS DELETED

I'M outside the only queer coffee shop in the city, waiting for Jamie to get us our coffees; mine with cream and sugar and his latte with cinnamon. I'm not allowed in after my latest outburst … calling the owner a fucking bigot, telling him he's using queer pride to make money.

In my defence, I was really fucking drunk. And I was right … but we still go back because the coffee is amazing.

"What's with that pissed-off look on your face?" Jamie jokingly demands as he comes out carrying my coffee and his latte with the sweet smell of cinnamon. He hands me my coffee with his gloved hand. It's getting cold in the city but I refuse to wear anything heavier than my black leather jacket.

"What's with your love-struck one?" I counter.

He raises an eyebrow at me. "I asked first. In the world of unwritten rules, you have to go first." Jamie purred.

"I was thinking of how I got kicked out of that shit-hole with the awesome coffee," I fake-growl. "That was fucking hilarious."

I watch Jamie's hazel eyes dance at the memory, "Now I can hit on guys when I'm there .," he says, his lips tugging up in a grin.

"You hit on them anyway."

He laughs. I love how his hazel eyes light up when he laughs. It actually makes me feel something. "Your turn," I said nudging him.

"I think I like Ben."

"Told you," I say triumphantly. "It helps that he is a cute as fuck." He fakes sighs.

"I fucking told you!" I say, punching Jamie in the shoulder.

He cringes and grabs his arm. "Fuck girl! You're stronger than you look. How's it going with your one-night stand?" He purrs, nudging me and waiting for my answer.

"You know I don't talk about that shit," I say my jaw tightening.

"Don't let that past shit with Melanie fuck your entire life," he says, almost kindly.

"It's not as easy as it sounds," I mutter, not looking at him.

"When I was in the tenth grade there was this super-hot guy named Tyler," Jamie sighs. "He was a junior. A *junior*, girl. He was always smiling and friendly … even to me. I thought he was flirting.

I asked him out." Jamie pauses, his body going tense, "And the football team promptly came and kicked my ass. So, I worked out and thank God got taller and eventually they left me the fuck alone. I'm good now. You can be too."

"Yeah but at least I'm not dating some guy to cover up the fact that I'm a fucking lesbian."

"How do you know that?" he demands.

"I kinda follow Melanie on Instagram," I say, purposely not looking at Jamie.

Jamie freezes in the middle of the street. "Give me your fucking phone."

"No !" I protest. He grabs it before I can move. He touches the screen and throws it back to me.

"I deleted her. Melanie and her beard have been deleted!" he screams.

People turn to look at us, some laughing, some shuffling away.

"The bitch and the beard are dead!"

"Shut the fuck up, Jamie!" I say, but I'm laughing too.

CHAPTER 11

SID AND NANCY IN THE BATHROOM

ANARCHY *in the U.K.* by the Sex Pistols is playing on Riot Radio. "For everyone who wants to fuck shit up tonight," I say over the air. Then I lean back and exhale slowly because the memories won't stop flooding my brain.

I'm running my tongue over this girls' teeth and her hand is grabbing my ass. I'm about to take off my pants when the door suddenly opens and slams against the wall. This butch girl with torn plaid and black jeans comes in, snarling. Her teeth are bared and her hands are clenched into fists.

"Get your hands off my girlfriend, you fucking slut!" she spits.

"Shit!" the girl says and gets off me like she's been burned.

"She came onto me!" I protest.

"Shut the fuck up!" she screams as her fist collides with my face. Pain explodes in my skull. I stagger back against the bathroom wall. I lean on the dirty tile to keep from falling. I try to stop the tears from coming. My whole body is shaking hard. I try to leave, thinking she's done with me but she grabs me hard. Her knee collides with my stomach. I gasp for air, pain exploding in every nerve. I try to push down a scream. Her fist breaks my nose as I clutch at my stomach. Blood gushes down and I fall to the floor. I gather all my anger and strength and manage to get back up. I punch her so hard that she staggers back and slams into the wall.

"Get the fuck out of here!" I say, clutching my stomach, blood dripping down my face. I watch her put her arm around her girlfriend and I sink to the floor as they leave.

My cell phone dings, saving me from drowning in the past again. It's Jamie. I ignore it.

"That was the Sex Pistols," I announce. "Now here is Jack White's one and only punk tune. *Fell in Love with a Girl.*" I sink into the couch, my hands gripping my face.

My phone dings again; it's Sophia. She wants to hang out tomorrow. Anything to make the memories stop. Anything. Even breaking my rule of never dating a one-night stand.

I say 'yes'.

The next day, Sophia and I go down the stairs of the black market and take in the freaks, the vintage clothes and all the shit they sell. I follow her to my favourite section, the leather jackets.

"In our line of business, you can never have too much leather," she says, grinning with those red painted lips and those blinding white teeth. It sounds kind of sexy in her French accent. I see a red one that looks like something an older Joan Jett would wear. I run my fingers over it … it's real leather!

"Here, try this." Her eyes light up, they are almost gold. She tries it on. "You look like fucking Joan Jett."

Her nose wrinkles up. "Yeah, the way she looks now. I want to look like when she was starting the punk revolution."

"Hey, looking like Joan is always a compliment. Take it. Take it and fucking run."

"I would, but then we might get caught for stealing this jacket," she laughs. I made her laugh. I want to hear it again. I want to be the one causing it. I think I'm falling for her. Shit!

I watch her consider a pile of t-shirts and her face makes a slow grin.

"It's a fucking Runaways shirt!" she says jumping on the balls of her feet. I bolt over, pushing past some hipster dude who looks way out of his depth. It says, 'The Runways' in red on a white tee, with the *Live in Japan* picture on it.

"We need this," she says.

"We need fucking ten!" I say.

We grab as many as we can and run, giggling like idiots. I watch her put a scarf around her neck and don some thick sunglasses.

"Charles, take my Shih Tzu to the vet or you're fired. I don't care if she bites," she says. I laugh as she struts around.

Then I see these boots. Purple docs with spikes on the heel. "Look at these!"

"Shit!" Sophia looks at me wide-eyed. "Check the size! Check the size!" she screams.

I frantically grab the tag. "Size seven!"

"I'm a size seven!"

"Fuck, me too!"

"We can share!" she says smiling.

I always hoard my finds, not letting anyone even *touch* them. Now I'm sharing these. Now I have someone who's more than just a fuck. Shit. I watch her grey eyes light up and her nose crinkle slightly. I want to take her and kiss her right now. Is this love?

We walk down the street laughing, fingers intertwined. Her grey eyes practically sparkling and lips wide with her smile. I never want to let go. I never want to let go. There's this tightness in my chest; I haven't felt like this since Melanie. This feeling ... it scares me. I have to tell myself that Sophia isn't Melanie. I won't end up crying in the dirt because she's a coward. I won't be broken-hearted.

But there's never a fucking guarantee.

"So, um ... does our band still have the guest spot on your show?

I freeze, my chest ice-cold. Is this why she's here? Was this all to get a gig for her fucking band? I stop and our hands fall apart. So I say out loud, "Is that what this is about? Your band getting the fucking gig?"

Her grey eyes flash, but with fury this time. "You don't trust me." It wasn't a question.

"I don't fucking know you!" I bark out.

"Fuck you," she shouts and stalks down the street in leather boots that I wish were mine.

"Your stupid band always had the gig!" I shout after her.

She just walks away shaking her head. Concrete this time, instead of gravel, but broken-hearted again.

CHAPTER 12

ISOLATION AND JOY DIVISION

I'M curled up in bed listening to *Joy Division* and shutting out the world. There's a knock on my door. I get up thinking it might be Ben or Jamie. No one else on this fucking planet would have a reason to knock on my door. I open the door to a blonde girl with a white tank and jeans. Blue eyes wide. Fuck. Like I could ever forget those blue eyes.

"Melanie?!" It feels like my whole world is crumbling underneath me. I desperately try to hold onto something, but it's too late.

"I was in the city," she says hesitantly. "I wanted to say hi."

Hi? After two fucking years, she wants to say 'hi'? That's it?

I feel my rage pulsing under my skin. "Where's your beard?" I spit out.

"What's wrong?" she murmurs. She comes closer and tucks my hair behind my ear. Just like she used to. She kisses me so softy. I want this … I want her … no … no not again!

I push her hard. She stumbles backward. I can't stand the look on her face. Like I hurt her first. "Get the fuck out!" Tears come suddenly, sobs heaving in my chest. "Get out of my apartment! Get the fuck out of my apartment!" Pain and sadness sear through me like a fire, burning my skin from the inside out. She grabs her purse and turns to leave, but first she looks at me with her huge blue eyes, tears forming.

"You're crying? You're crying?" I sputter. I watch her run down the hallway, my fists clenched, my knuckles turning white.

"Yeah, you better run!" I hear Sophia scream. She has appeared in the hallway and now she turns to me wearing a dirty-white towel on her head and a worn-out, turquoise bathrobe. "What the fuck is going on?" she asks, her grey eyes searching my face.

"An ex," I mutter turning my head away. I don't want Sophia to see the tears. I don't want someone I fucked to see the tears. She follows me to my apartment.

"Yeah, I gathered that. You want me to slash her tires for you? Break her nose ?" I watch her search my face for the answer.

"Ha." I let out a bitter laugh. "Fucking tempting." The burn from seeing Melanie again leaves a hole, gaping, sore and raw.

"What the fuck happened between you two ?"

"She's not really gay," I mutter. A coward still after all these years.

She scrunches her nose, "Those are the worst. Definitely slashing her tires." She pauses, "Girl, I have a business proposition for you."

"I'm listening."

"My band plays your radio station tomorrow night! What do you say?"

"Hmm. I've always wanted a live band to play at the station," I said playfully. As if this hadn't already been in the works. "How much do you want?" I ask.

"Whatever, we just want exposure," she says the words like she's eating them, like she's hungry. It's like the conversation that left me broken-hearted on the concrete never fucking happened.

"What should we play? Covers? Originals?" she asks exposing those blinding white teeth.

I think about it for a minute. All covers, people won't take you seriously as a band—all originals and people get bored. "Both. Definitely both," I say. Then, "Hey, my one friend wants to meet you."

She laughs. "Not *a* friend? One friend?"

"I literally have one friend," I say, using laughter to hide my pain.

She rewards me with a laugh. It's like we are putting all that shit that happened earlier behind us. Punks hold grudges … I'm not used to this … forgiveness.

"What's your friend like ?" she asks.

"He's covered in tattoos, a secret hipster and as gay as fuck."

"Good, I know too many straight people," she says, rolling her eyes.

"We all know too many straight people. Come out queers … stop hiding you little shits!" I say, like I'm drunk or high or like I'm not really here.

"Get the fuck out of the closet and party with us!" Sophia screams. Like she is drunk or high or not really here. Laughter colours our faces. She kisses me, laughing, rolling on the bed … and you can figure the rest out from here.

CHAPTER 13

BANDS AND ASSHOLES

I'M at Riot Radio playing *Trans Soul Rebel* by Against Me!. I'm getting shit from transphobic assholes and I'm throwing their shit right back in their fucking faces. I don't give a fuck if they stop listening.

"If you are transphobic or homophobic and listening to Riot Radio I will happily hunt you down and kick your ass myself," I snarl over the air. The board lights up. "You're on Riot Radio."

"Tom Gabel turned out to be a fucking fag." Tom Gabel is Laura Jane Grace's dead name.

"And you turned out to be a shit for brains. Crawl in a fucking hole," I spit.

"Bitch."

I laugh. "You got that right."

"Now an up-and-coming punk band is going to play a set for us. But first, *Glad to be Gay* by the Tom Robinson band. Fuck you, all you assholes!" I snarl.

I hear the door open and a bunch of punks comes in with smiles and white teeth.

"Sasha!" Sophia says.

"Hello, luv." She comes and hugs me. I stiffly hug her back. I'm not used to this, seeing the person I fuck outside the bedroom. But Sophia is more than that now.

"So, you're little Sasha," says this tall guy with kind, brown eyes and brown hair hanging past his neck. He is wearing a worn band shirt with holes, a jean vest and red and black pants.

"Who the fuck says I'm little?" I shoot back. He laughs, his eyes lighting up. My chest tightens. I've always loved making people's eyes light up; it's more fucking real than a smile—smiles lie, eyes don't.

"We'll just set up back here," Sophia says. He leans back and takes me in.

"You going to help them?" I ask.

"I'm the lead guitarist. I can't afford to damage my fingers," he says wiggling his fingers.

"That's Andy. He's an asshole and we love him," Sophia says with affection.

"I am," he says, revealing perfect teeth.

"How did a kid get her own radio station anyway?" I cringe at the word 'kid'. I'm more fucking accomplished than most adults.

"Luck," I say, and nothing more.

I never know what people want from me; I don't know what he wants from an eighteen-year-old, awkward lesbian.

"Andy get your ass over here," someone says. I take in the bassist.

He's got a blonde fauxhawk, ugly face and a drunken sneer. I know him … the blonde Sid Vicious I saw at the club the day I got kicked out. He plays fucking bass just like the fated poster boy of punk himself.

I shake the shivers off me and watch them set up amps and wires and tune their guitars. When Sophia gives me the okay signal and a huge grin, I go on the air. "Now we have the up-and-coming punk band, Velvet Rage. I'll let them take it from here!"

Andy goes to the mic. "We are Velvet Rage and this is *Red Painted Lips*." Andy starts playing a riff on a red Gibson, his head hanging like he is blocking out the whole world. The drummer's beat is fast and insistent—but the bassist is sloppy and missing notes.

I may not play an instrument but I know fucking know music. I also know what it looks like to be drunk and high out of your fucking mind. Sophia sways in front of the mic like she can't tell he's fucking up. Her eyes are wide open and she is grinning.

> *Your red painted lips suck what's left of my soul.*
> *Red-painted lips who do they belong to now?*
> *Red-painted lips bring me down.*
> *Red-painted lips bring me down.*

Andy comes in on vocals for '*bring me down*'.

"Fuck, fuck can we start again?" The blonde bass player is fumbling, looking like he's lost his place.

"Um, we're live," Andy says.

"Shit … shit fuck. Stop it!"

"Get us off the air!" Andy signals to me to cut it.

"Hey, weirdos we're taking a quick break," I say. "Here's our queen, Kathleen Hanna." I play *Rebel Girl* and turn back to the band.

Andy is looking away from the band, his jaw tight. The drummer is pretending to fix his drums. Sophia is biting her lip. Rage pushes against my skull trying to find its way out.

"What the fuck is wrong with you?" I say to the bass player. Everyone turns their eyes towards me. "I give you this fucking gig and you come drunk and high? You probably fucking cost me listeners. You shouldn't be in the fucking band if you can't take it seriously."

"You don't know fucking anything about me," he sneers. "All you do is press a fucking button for a living." His face is becoming red and veins are popping on his neck. He comes closer to me. My body tenses, ready to fight, ready to kick his little ass. He comes up

to me swaying and gets right into my face. I can smell the booze
and I can see the sweat and grease on his face. His face has hard
lines and infected sliver piercings. I force myself not to move, not
to show the fear growing in my stomach.

"I formed this band. You're just a little bitch," he spits as he talks.

"Fuck you, you drunk asshole." I see his hand reaching to hit me.
I gather all the strength I have and I punch him in the face first. He
pulls back, his nose bloody.

"You little bitch!" he screams as Andy holds him back. He
thrashes and tries to spit at me.

"Come on, brother. Leave her alone," Andy says, his voice tight.

Brother!? That's why he's still in the fucking band. That's
Andy's brother.!

"Let go of me! Let go of me!" he shouts. I back up as far as I can,
fear rushing through my veins.

"Sasha, you should have stayed out of it." I look to see dis-
appointment written all over Sophia's face. Her huge grey eyes
look exhausted.

"That's Andy's brother. Do you know how hard it is to find
a fucking bassist?" She shakes her head hard. "He's fine when he's
is not drunk out of this mind. Just stay away." They quickly pack
up and leave with Andy steering his fuming brother out the door.

It feels like my lungs are giving in. I can't breathe. My studio
is starting to spin. I reach out to steady myself. I fall back on the
black velvet couch. I take a bottle out from under the couch without
thinking about it. I open it with my teeth. The bassist isn't the only
one who can get fucked up. I let the drink run down my throat.
I put a whole album on the turntable so I can keep pounding the
booze and I don't stop until everything is hazy. Until the room is
spinning and I can't think anymore.

I stagger over to the mic and go on the air. "Never fucking trust
anyone! They will stab you in the fucking front. Be stone cold. Be
a bitch." My words slur, but I mean every one of them. "My so-called

friend chose her fucking bassist over me. She's a fake. Never help anyone, ever. Just look out for yourself."

As sobs catch in my throat, I announce over the airways "And Velvet Rage is a shitty band. Never listen to them. They are posers. Please enjoy *Love Kills* by Joey Strummer."

The next morning, I open the door to my building, coffee in one hand and my notebook in the other. I'm almost at my apartment door when I hear someone approaching.

"Hey! Hey!" It takes me a minute to understand that the 'hey' is for me. I turn and it feels like the ground is caving in underneath me. It's Sophia. Everything in me is telling me to run.

"What the fuck did you say about my band?" she's screaming, her eyes wild and her fists clenched tight at her side. She is moving quickly towards me and I want to break down right there. I can feel it coming, the anxiety spreading and crawling under my skin, the sadness presses behind my skull threatening to take me under. What have I done? What the fuck have I done? Her eyes are blazing, her mouth tight. She looks like she wants to tear me apart right fucking here.

"Let's talk inside," I say quietly. That way only one person can see me fall apart. She follows me in. "I'm so fucking sorry." My throat clenches to keep the sobs from exploding. "I was really drunk." I choke out a sob and it catches in my throat.

"No club is going to take us now! Do you fucking realize that?" she is screeching, tears staining her face and her fists shaking.

"I'll apologize on the air. I'll go right now." I sound so desperate. I hate being this desperate. I hate it.

"Won't make a difference. It's done now."

"I was just trying to stand up for you. He was fucking up the song, even I could see that."

"Don't do it again!" she says.

I let the tears fall now, hard.

"Please give me another chance." I'm begging. I'm fucking begging. "I'm sorry."

"I'm sorry I was being such a bitch," she sighs, rubbing her face with her hand.

"No, I …" I start.

"Let me finish," she says, her voice firm. I never heard Sophia like this. "The band is everything to me. We are sacking Chris the bassist. You're right, he's shit. You don't play bass by any chance, do you?" she looks up at me, hopeful.

"No, sorry. But I know someone who does."

Sophia 's eyes light up. "Are they any good?"

"Um yeah, I think so."

"Screw it, whoever it is we'll take them."

"Um, I'll call him right now." I pull out my phone and call Jamie.

"Hey."

"Hey, girl. Spill … why you calling?"

"What, I can't call to say hi?"

"That's what texting is for, luv."

"You free right now?"

"Besides painting my nails a shiny blue? Yes."

"You wanna join a band?"

"Are you thinking of starting a band?"

"No, um, Sophia's band needs a bassist."

"And Sophia is?"

"Uh … a friend."

"I'll be there in ten for you girl."

"Thanks, you're a lifesaver."

"I know."

"He's coming," I say to Sophia.

"Oh, thank God," she sighs.

"You think he'll want to join the band?" she asks as she looks expectantly at me for an answer.

"He's got nothing else to do."

She laughs. I do it without thinking. I lean in and kiss her. I let her hand trail down my back. I wrap my hands around her waist.

I want this. I want this. She's playing with the back of my bra when the door opens. Jamie stops in the doorway.

"Shit Jamie, don't you knock?" His eyebrows rise and he gives his signature twisted grin.

"You must be the bassist that is going to save our asses. I'm Sophia." She sticks out hand. Jamie just stares at it observing the chipped silver polish. "Shake my fucking hand and let's get on with it." She laughs.

"Um … okay." he says. I've never seen Jamie off his game, I'm enjoying this.

I notice a new tattoo on Jamie's arm as he tunes up his bass. I just hope Jamie is good as I think he is. Anything will be fucking better than that blonde slop trying to be Sid Vicious.

"You want a punk beat or something more complicated?" he asks.

"More complicated," Sophia says, shoulders back and head up like she's royalty and she's ordering her musicians to play for her. Jamie nods and starts playing the bass line for *Psycho Killer* by the Talking Heads. He doesn't miss a note. I watch Sophia's face, trying to gauge what she is thinking. He's fucking better than the blonde Sid they had and I know Jamie would never show up fucking drunk to a gig.

I keep getting comments on how shitty Velvet Rage was on Riot Radio. What will happen if I give them another chance? I might lose a lot of fucking listeners. I shake the thoughts from setting roots in my brain. I fucking owe them for the shit I said. They're not shit, it was their fucking bassist.

After Jamie finishes his riff, I watch Sophia go up to him and extend her hand. He looks disapprovingly at her chipped nails. "Welcome to Velvet Rage," she says. A grin splits across his face. I have to push down the jealousy that is searing through me. I'm usually the only one that can get Jamie to smile, really smile. I try to shake the feeling away but it sticks to my insides.

"I'm going introduce him to the rest of the band," Sophia says, pulling me back to reality. "You want to come?"

I shake my head. "I'll stay here and then go to Riot Radio."

"Okay see you later." She says happily.

"Bye, stay out of trouble girl," Jamie says with that lazy smile that I know means trouble.

"You know that's impossible," I say and for a moment it was just me and Jamie again the way it should be.

"You're going to love the band," Sophia says. Her words cut through me. They won't need me.

"Hey, all you freaks out there … you probably guessed how fucking drunk I was the last time I was on the air," I say. "I said some shitty things about Velvet Rage. They aren't posers—they have real talent and they finally just got a good bass player. Speaking of fucked-up bass players, here is Sid Vicious singing *I Wanna Be Your Dog.*"

I shut my eyes, memories pulsing behind them in the dark. The smell is what I remember first. The apartment stinks of sweat and booze. Bottles take up most of the floor competing with piles of vinyl and CDs. I haven't gotten out of bed for days. There is no point. I have enough bottles to last for weeks and an endless selection of music to listen to. My limbs feel heavy, my mind is in a thick, never-ending fog. I feel flat, numb like I can't move. I am not motivated to do anything. It has been weeks since I showered. My clothes and breath stink of booze. My skin is greasy and covered in sweat.

It was a Japanese import that saved my life. On one of the rare days when I managed to lift myself up and scroll through my computer, I was looking at record stores and one site said a bunch of Joan Jett Japanese imports had just come in.

I go to the bathroom and wash my face with ice cold water. Sasha save yourself before it's too late, a voice in the back of my mind tells me. I put on foundation with a shaky hand and comb my hair with a wet brush. I put on some deodorant, some jeans, a tee and a denim jacket. I put on my docs before I convince myself not to leave the apartment. I grab my backpack and go.

Before I know it, I'm in front of the store. It's nothing special, just a small store that says Riot Records in fading black and red paint. I open the door and step in. There is a man behind the counter who reminds me of Rick. He has long grey hair and a thick white beard. He's wearing a denim jacket and a fading Iggy Pop t-shirt.

"Hey, can I help you?" he says, his smile revealing yellow, decaying teeth.

"Yeah. I read online that you have some Joan Jett Japanese imports."

"Yeah, we just got those in. Some Runaways, too."

"Fuck, are you serious?" My jaw literally falls open.

He laughed. "I'm serious." Revealing his decaying teeth again. "I'm a bit of a Joan Jett freak. It's nice to meet another one," he says.

His words barely process in my brain. Fucking Joan Jett and Runaways Japanese imports. That's fucking gold to a Joan Jett die-hard.

"Can I see them?" I ask. I want to see them in person. He takes a pile of records from the shelf. I take in a picture of the Runaways I've never seen and I thought I had seen them all. It's the lead singer Cherie Currie in her infamous black and white corset;

Joan Jett in her red and black leather jumper, looking moody behind her gold Les Paul; Lita Ford—the lead guitarist—in her black and sliver shorts, her long red-brown hair covering most of her face; Sandy West, the drummer, grinning behind her set; and, you can just make out the bassist Jackie Fox in the background.

I trail my hand on the import sleeve. I go through the piles and see Joan Jett stretched out, in all leather, daring the world to fuck with her. "How much for all of them?" I ask.

Suddenly my eyes fly open because the song ends and dead air is about to begin. I stagger to the mic, back in my real world.

"Since there is no asshole breathing down my neck, telling me what to play, I'm going to play Joan Jett singing *I Wanna Be Your Dog*. I really don't give a fuck if you have a problem with it. Go listen to some mainstream shit then because I don't give a fuck."

After the show Jamie comes by to walk me home. I stop. I'm kind of fucked up. "I need a smoke," I say.

I'm taking a drag of my cigarette, trying to still the shaking in my hand. I'm leaning against a brick wall, the roughness digging into my back. Jamie smokes, too. He takes a drag, watching me with those painted hazel eyes flecked with bits of gold. I exhale slowly watching the smoke disappear.

"What's up with you?" he asks.

"Fucking nothing," I spit.

Jamie sighs and rubs his eyes. "I've known you for too long, girl. I know when something's wrong."

"You and Sophia are going to be spending all your time together," I say with a shaky voice.

"You do realize we're both fucking gay, right? We're not going to become girlfriend and boyfriend," he says mockingly. "And we're definitely not going to fuck."

"I mean I'll have no one." I mutter, my eyes boring into the dirty concrete ground.

"Do you want us to end up like you?"

"What?" The words cut like a dagger, sharp and searing. My eyes widen and I hope I heard him wrong. I hope he didn't say those words to me.

"Doing nothing with your life?" he fixes me with a cold glare.

"You think Riot Radio is nothing? I built a successful station from fucking nothing." I spit. Venom edging into my words. I can feel the rage pulsing behind my eyes. The fire licking my bones.

"It's not like you make any money. You're never going to be anything." Jamie spits back. "You are going to live in your dirty, tiny apartment for the rest of your life, scrounging for change for a fucking coffee," he says, sneering down at me.

I've heard that before, it sticks to my thoughts. You won't ever be anything. You will never be anything. I will myself not to disappear into the past. It's just so fucking hard.

"I have to be something ?" I scream, letting my rage go full-force against him instead of myself. "You fucking poser!" I can feel my skin redden and my whole body shakes with rage. "With your stupid fucking alt coffee shops and your fucking vintage clothes and saying you'll never being a slave to a job. It's all lies! It's all bullshit! Fuck you! I never want to see your face again!"

"Sasha!" he grabs my arm. Pain shoots up my arm. I feel tears stinging my eyes.

"Let go of me!" I scream so fucking loud he drops my arm. I pull away and run back to my apartment. I open the door, shaking hard. I can barely breathe. My world is crumbling around me and this time I have nothing to stop myself from destroying it. It feels like the walls are crumbling, everything holding me together is leaving me. Fear is eating away at me, it feels like pure desperation. I'm strung out and shaking all over. I can't think, I just need the pain to stop. I grab my knees and let the tears come down. Fucking poser! Fake!

Fucking fake. Rage pours in, giving strength to my shaking legs. I grab my CDs and throw them against the wall, over and over until I hear them break. Fresh rage appears with every one I pick up. Tears fall down and snot runs down to my mouth. I watch the CDs shatter as they hit the wall. My whole body shakes. I scream, letting the sound rip out of my lungs until my throat is sore. I find myself picking up the Runaways Japanese import, ready to throw it. No, not this one. Not this one. I sink to the floor and clutch it to my chest. A Japanese import saved my life again.

I wake up, my eyes sore and puffy, my throat sore from crying. I get up, peeling myself off the floor. I stagger upright and take in the damage. Sobs catch in my throat. My CDs are in pieces. I worked so hard to find these. I fall to my knees, unable to breathe. What the fuck have I done? This sadness is choking me. I struggle to get air into my lungs. I frantically look around for the Joan Jett and Runways CDs—those will be impossible to replace. I find one after the other, thankfully untouched.

I try to breathe, but I feel I can't. The room is spinning. My stomach is churning and I heave vomit onto the floor. Fresh tears come down my face again. There's a knock on the door. Jamie? Hope rushes through me. I hastily wipe my mouth and the tears off my face. I stagger as fast as I can and whip the door open. My heart sinks when I see it's not Jamie. It's my neighbour, Ben.

"Ben, what do you want?" His blue eyes widen and a blush creeps up on his face.

"Um … I uh … heard crying. I … uh … just wanted to see if you were okay." I watch him take in the destruction I created last night. His eyes are pained like he knows me enough to care.

"You got anything to drink?" I ask, desperate.

"I … uh … don't think I should give you anything to drink right now," he mumbles nervously.

"Just give me something to drink!" I scream in his face. "Fuck you, just give me a fucking drink!"

He looks terrified, but he still shakes his head.

"I'm not okay Ben. I'm not okay." I sob as I sink to the floor clutching my knees. To my surprise, he wraps his arms around me and I bury my head in his shoulder.

He takes me into his apartment and sits me down on his cream coloured sofa covered with faded roses. He wraps a thick blanket around me and I settle into the softness. I watch him move around the kitchen, putting a kettle on. Minutes later he hands me a mug with a tea bag. I take the cup, my hands shaking hard. I will them to settle, but the anxiety is flowing through me like rough waves destroying everything in its path. I feel something warm around my hands. I open my eyes to Ben's hands wrapped around mine. "Ben?"

"Yeah ?" he says. I have to look away from his eyes. He's trying to figure what kind of fucked up I am.

"Do you want a job?" I ask him.

"I'd love one. Did you ... did you just get fired? Is that ... is that ..."

"Why I broke down?" I say matter-of-factly. "No," I whisper. I want to say Jamie's name, and in the same whisper tell Ben what a poser he is, but I can't do that to him. Ben likes Jamie and I don't want to destroy that for him. He's too ... good.

"It doesn't pay well," I say. My eyes scanning his face for his answer. He gives me a weak smile. "I'll take anything at this point. I can't go back home."

"What's going on at home?" For a moment I think Ben is going to pull a Sasha and break down right in front of me. Fuck, I hope not. I'm no good at putting the pieces back together unless they're my own.

"Some people want me dead," he whispers, tears choking his words.

"What! Do you owe money to a loan shark or something?" I get a small satisfaction from his tight smile.

"I kissed a football player ... He, um ... we were kind of dating. He, um ... freaked out because some of his teammates saw us kissing. He freaked out, screaming that I came on to him. That I was a fucking pervert." I watch Ben tighten his grip on the couch.

He said staring at me with tears in those blue eyes. For some reason, I want to hold him and tell its all going to be okay and then hunt this guy down and kick his lying ass. I didn't think I cared about Ben this much, but I guess I do.

Shit, the exact thing happened to Jamie. I guess asshole football playing homophobic asshole's are more common than I thought.

"Try being in love and then when the parents find out, she's straight and says I came on to *her*." I share.

"We're both a cliché," he laughs. It feels like a fucking victory to make him smile.

"What about this job?" he asks.

"Meet me at eight at my apartment." I get up feeling exposed suddenly without the blanket. "Thanks for the tea."

"Wait … you don't have to go," he protests. "I um … Don't go," he says.

"Okay," I whisper.

As I lay awake in Ben's apartment on his dated couch I swear to myself to leave Jamie and Sophia behind. They are fucking toxic and getting in the way of my dream. No one is walking over me again and making me feel worthless, like I'm nothing. I'm too busy for that. I have a radio station to run. Fuck you both.

You guys are probably wondering how a punk kid with issues got a radio station. I'll indulge you a bit and tell you all about it.

I'm leaning against the counter looking at the Runaways Japanese imports at Riot Records and I look up to see the store owner grinning at me.

"It's cool to find another hard core Runaways fan. There's not too many of us around. People think that they are just some punk kids and girls at that."

"That's the beauty. They are just punk kids," I say smirking. He chuckles, but it sounds more like a wheezing cough.

"What's your name kid?"

"Sasha."

"I'm Bill."

"What do you do Sasha?"

"Not much just moved to the city."

"You wanna a job?" he says wheezing again.

"Are you kidding me ?" I ask. I just fucking met this guy. Is he hiring me just because I'm a fucking Runaways die-hard ?

"No kidding Sasha, he wheezes again. "I'm getting old. And I'll give you a discount on the Runways and Joan Jett vinyl."

"Sold," I say.

"Come by tomorrow at 8:00," he says.

"Got it captain," I say leaving the store.

The next morning I'm at the store blurry eyed with coffee in hand. Bill is outside having a smoke.

"Those things will kill you, you know,"I say smirking.

"You want one?" he says extending a cigarette towards me.

"Yep."

I take a long drag and then take a sip of my latte.

"Who's your favourite Runaway? he asks. Mines's Cherie."

"Joan Jett hands down," I say.

"She is definitely the most successful," says Bill.

"For a good reason too. Plus, she's hot," I say.

I don't care if he knows I'm gay. I don't need to fucking hide it.

Bill laughs and wheezes, "Let's get to work."

Turns out I was a fucking natural. I picked up the record lingo right away.

A 33 is a full length album and a 45 has a single on it. A gate fold is a record that opens to reveal a picture. The thicker the record the better the quality.

I became a record buyer in a matter of weeks which means when someone came in with an album to sell, I could determine right away if it was shit or not and worth adding to our collection.

A typical conversation with Bill went something like this:

"Why is Cherie Currie your favourite Runaway?" I'd ask. I know that's his favourite subject. I watch his eyes sparkle and the wrinkles around his eyes crease deeply.

"She wasn't the greatest singer but she really put herself out there. That takes guts, he wheezes.Plus she wore a fucking corset. Who did that?"

"Why do you like Joan?" he'd ask.

"She's was a fucking badass with her punk leather jacket. Plus she helped start the fucking punk movement, I'd reply. And she helped write the songs. She had talent."

"But we can both agree Kim Fowley was an asshole manager right?" he says grinning.

"Yes we can," I laugh.

A few months later I got the crushing news that Bill died suddenly from a massive heart attack.

I sat in the back at the funeral wearing a black tank and my black skinny jeans. My shoulders shaking with sobs, my eyeliner smearing my face. He was my only friend here, without him and the job I'm fucking alone. I'm so alone.

It was a fucking surprise when I was told to come to the reading of Bill's will. When I got there I froze in the doorway. My chest became tight and tears started to burn in my eyes. There were Bill's children. No tears coming from their eyes. My rage started to build. He would say how proud he was of them even though they didn't talk to him anymore. How dare they not fucking cry over him. My hands tightened into fists. Bill was a kind, funny and intelligent person. How dare they not cry over him. I slip in and take a seat making sure to give his kids a full glare as I sit down. I can barely pay attention to the will reading. Sadness is choking my throat and I'm starting to feel dizzy. I'm really fucking nervous. I shouldn't be here.

"And I will leave the record store to Sasha Miller because I know she is the only one who would want it and loves Cherie Currie and Joan Jett as much as I do," Bill's will read.

"Wait! What?" Bill's kids and I said at the same time.

"Can you…can you say that again?" I manage to sputter out.

"Are you Sasha Miller ?" asks the executor.

"Uh ..yeah." I reply, my voice shaking.

"You now own Riot Records," he announces.

I grip the chair to keep from fucking fainting in front of everyone. Shit. I own Riot Records and I know just what to do with it. Get ready for Riot Radio. The greatest independent radio station in the world.

CHAPTER 14

BEN, I CAN'T REALLY PAY YOU (THAT MUCH)

I start to wake up on Ben's couch enjoying the softness of the blanket around me. I stay there for a moment not wanting to move, not wanting to go back to reality. I fumble for my phone, only half awake. I look and it says 7:45 a.m. Fuck. Shit. I throw the blanket off about to scramble to get my things together … then I realize this is not my place.

"Ben! Wake up! Wake the fuck up!" He springs up from the floor where he's been sleeping beside me, his eyelids half closed.

"What do you want for breakfast?" he asks, sleep still sticking to his words.

"Screw breakfast, we're going to be late!"

"How pissed will the boss be?" Ben asks, his eyes widening with anxiety. I stretch my arms out.

"You're fucking looking at her!" Ben just stares at me wide-eyed and his mouth hangs open. "And you have to open up!"

That didn't take long. Usually, it takes people a fucking long time to understand I'm the fucking boss of anything.

"Shit, sorry let's go!" he says.

"We gotta go to my place. I need my laptop." I rush into my place, grab my laptop and phone and we scramble down the stairs. "Let's go!" We book it to Queen Street East.

"I own a radio station," I say between breaths. "You'll sort records and give me suggestions about what to play." I add, "Sometimes, if I ask."

"Fine with me."

I stop abruptly. "This is it."

Ben skids to a stop. I open the iron door and then the main door. We go inside and I widen my arms and grin. "Welcome, freaks and weirdos, to Riot Radio!"

"Where's everyone else? Not here yet?"

"Ben, I hate to break it to you, but we're everyone." I watch him sigh. I tense for a moment. Shit. He's going to back out, find a real job.

"That's great, I really don't like people."

"Sweet, neither do I," I grin. "First order of business, make yourself a coffee and pick songs that say, 'fuck the world'."

"Got it."

"I hate to ask, but how are you going to pay me?"

"Don't be afraid to ask me that Benjamin," I say.

"I have a lot of rare records. I will sell them every few weeks to pay you. But it won't be much," I warn.

"Better than staying at home," he said smirking.

"That's the spirit Benjamin," I say.

I press the button. We are on the air. "Hello, insomniacs and die-hard listeners. I dub this day 'kick posers in the ass day'. Go out there and kick a poser in the ass!"

Then I say, "Tell me the story about kicking a poser's ass and we'll play a request. That's right, today Riot Radio is fucking taking requests."

The buttons light up right away.

"You're on the air."

"I'm a fucking fan. I listen to you all time, especially in class. Stops me from fucking banging my head on my desk."

"Whose ass did you kick today?"

"These girls wearing Nirvana shirts and flannel all the time thinking they are so fucking cool. I called them out on it and they didn't know a single fucking Nirvana song."

"What song you want to hear?"

"*Rebel Girl* by Bikini Kill."

"Consider it done."

I put the song on and I go off the air.

"Ben, your first test!" He looks up from sorting the records. "Get me the Bikini Kill singles album!" He just continues to stare at me, wide-eyed. "You don't know what I'm fucking talking about do you?"

He shakes his head. "Am … I … Am I fired?" I watch him tap his fingers frantically on the desk.

"Fuck no! I get to teach you about Bikini Kill. You don't understand, Ben! I've been waiting for this moment." I'm restless. I fucking love knowing more about music than the next person and it's even better when you get to rub it in their face. Not that I'm going to rub it in Ben's face, he's too fucking nice.

"You've been waiting patiently your whole life to teach someone about Bikini Kill?" he asks with a teasing grin.

"Fuck yeah!" I go over to the turntable and put the song on. "Sit down and get ready for a crash course," I say, grinning. "It all started with Kathleen Hanna. She was into feminist poetry and met her feminist idol who told her that people don't listen to poetry, they listen to bands. Hanna met with other revolutionaries that were into feminism and wanted to put that into their art. Hanna met with Alison Wolfe and decided to start a whole fucking do-it-yourself feminist movement. They both formed bands and started singing about all the shit women go through. They made zines, they had meetings. They called it Riot Grrrl and at the forefront was Hanna's band, Bikini Kill."

"Thank you, wise one," Ben said, grinning and bowing to me.

"There's a lot where that comes from, young Benji," I say, my smile splitting my face.

I straighten my back, stick out my chin and go back into boss lady mode. "Ben keep sorting shit. I'm gonna see if any more requests come in."

The red button is flashing. I grin because that means I'm a successful little bitch. I'm taking the word bitch back, by the way.

"You're on the air."

"I just stood up to the jocks today, calling them idiots. Thinking they're big shots, picking on kids smaller than them. I got my ass kicked, but it was worth it."

"And what is your request on 'kick posers in the ass day'?"

"Um ... you guys are on Queen Street East, right?"

"Why, you coming to complain? Because I'll kick your ass."

"Uh no, I want to quit school. If I go back they will kill me. I need a job. You hiring?"

Fuck, no. I can fucking barely afford Ben. Images bleed through my mind of this scrawny punk kid getting his face beaten in by jocks because I didn't fucking say yes.

"Come in for an interview, tomorrow at noon. Number 111."

"Sweet, thanks!" His voice full of relief.

"You didn't get the job yet," I say, pressing the button to get us off the air.

"Ben grab Iggy Pop, *Raw Power*. I wanna play the first side."

"Right now?"

"Fuck, yes. Half my listeners only listen cuz I don't talk the whole fucking time."

"Okay." He hands me the album. Those eyes are searching me, trying to understand me, but I won't let them.

"I'm gonna rest," I say, "Keep sorting and take a break whenever you want. Grab food or something."

"You want anything boss?"

"Get the boss lady a bagel with cream cheese. I'll pay you when you get back," I say.

"Forget about it," Ben says as the door slams behind him.

I close my eyes and she's back-Sonia with her willowy, pale limbs and her golden, blonde hair down to her hips. Her easy, perfect, pink smile and her pale blue eyes always electrify me. She's wearing a Riot Grrrl white crop top and low-slung jeans and we're stealing kisses in the feminist bookstore she worked in. Her hands trailing my body, prickling electricity on my skin. My lips part in a moan against hers. She pulls back suddenly and I freeze like ice water is shooting through my veins. I thought she was all mine. This perfect girl, all mine. It was a fucking lie.

"Hey, it's time. Lets go." Beth comes in with her dirty blonde mohawk and worn leather jacket. You can smell her before she even arrives. Revolutionaries don't fucking shower, I guess. I watch her brown eyes narrow in disapproval. She disapproves of anything that interrupts the cause. We follow her outside and join the Riot Grrrl march against people charged with sexual assault. I should have run then. I should have just fucking run. Kathleen never meant for her movement turn like this-violent.

The girls are angry. They spit slogans, their faces twisted in waves of disgust and fury. There's something in the air, it feels like this tension will break at any moment. That can only mean bloodshed. Dread grows in my stomach, tight and insistent. I see Sonia, her beautiful face turned ugly and Beth, anger oozing from every single pore. She'll kick my ass if

I run, or worse. I'm holding a sign that says Pussy Grabs Back! I'm screaming the slogan at the top of my lungs.

I look at an endless sea of mohawks and dyed hair, faded blues, purples. Worn leather jackets and snarls from pierced and tattooed faces. I hear sirens and my dread spreads to every limb, but we keep going. Then I see the police and everything turn to shit.

I hear it before I see it. The sound of glass shattering. It covers the ground and it sparkles in the afternoon sun. It's the girls hurling rocks into windows. Kathleen wouldn't have wanted this. What the fuck have we done? I'm shaking, guilt and raw fear make me feel like I'm going to fucking throw up.

I can't move, it's like I'm stuck in a nightmare. Police are spreading like a fucking disease grabbing girls by the waist. Horrible howling screams split through the air as they thrash in their holds. My sisters, being treated like fucking animals because we want our rights.

My rage is drowning in the screams inside me that are telling me to run and save myself. It's like a fucking dream. Girls twisting in the arms of the police, tears and screams all bleeding into one. Girls on their knees, crying out because of the shiny black boots on their backs. The smell of pepper spray floats through the air. I look desperately for Sonia. My heart is beating too hard in my chest and panic is screaming white in my brain. I'm terrified that she's one of the girls in the hold. Imagining someone bruising the face that makes me want to be a better person. I see her. Relief pours in and I'm about to scream her name. Then the world shifts under my feet. I see her grabbing hold of another girl and kissing her desperately, as if it's the last kiss. I scream and then arms are around me trying to shove me to the ground. I struggle hard. I'm not going down without a fight. All my rage is on the surface now. I want to kick, tear, bite and scratch. Anything to make him hurt. His arms are too tight, I can feel my ribs crushing inside me.

Tears stream down my face as I scream, "I'm not an animal! I'm not a fucking animal! Fuck you!" I kick him hard with all the strength I have left. I break free only to be kicked to the ground. I clutch my stomach as the pain explodes through me. The asphalt seems to be spinning. Those fuckers. I feel another kick. I can't even scream. There's no point, nothing to fight for. I close my eyes waiting for it to be over.

My eyes fly open. I get up. I'm shaking. I take off Iggy Pop and play this rare copy of a girl singing *Let's Start a Riot* by Three Days Grace. The door opens and Ben comes in.

"Here's your bagel," he says, grinning. I sigh, taking in his niceness, his warmth. "I made sure they put on extra cream cheese."

"Thanks," I murmur.

"Hey, you okay?" he asks with those eyes, trying to understand. I can't let that happen.

"Uh yeah. Let's sort out a place for the job interview."

We move piles and piles of records and set up a desk with two chairs. The rest of the day I'm teaching Ben how to use the buttons on the control panel and giving him crash courses on punk bands he's never heard of. I usually stay at Riot Radio 'till one in the morning. It's the time when I have the most listeners—that time when punks and freaks say, 'fuck the world' and 'fuck sleep', but I want to be at least semi-awake for the interview tomorrow.

"Aren't you ever scared to walk home at one in the morning?" Ben asks as we walk home together.

"Fuck no, I've been through worse. Besides Jamie would walk with me a lot." I hate the hurt in my voice as I say his name. Angry flames lick my insides. Pissed at what he really is.

"What happened, Sasha? Last night?"

I keep walking. Ben grabs my arms, more gently than anyone ever has.

"Jamie … he … he … told me that he never wants to be like me. Doing nothing with his life." My voice is shaking now. "Like Riot Radio is nothing. Doesn't he know how hard it is to fucking find records and the songs to play and work from eight in the morning to one in the morning? Or how it feels to deal with death threats because some asshole didn't like the song or band I played? Fuck him!"

Hot tears gather in my eyes. "I'm sorry. I shouldn't be telling you this. Fuck. You like him." I look away. I can't remember the last time I let someone see me cry.

"Not anymore." he murmurs. "He sounds like an ass."

"Yeah, he is. Let's go get some sleep so we can give a good interview tomorrow," I say, shutting down the conversation.

"K." I know Ben wants to hear more, but there's nothing more to say.

I'm about to fall asleep when I hear pounding on my apartment door. I bolt up, panicked. Cold sweat suddenly sticking to my skin. Should I open the door? Who would want to talk to me this bad?

I open the door and it's Jamie. Fuck. And he's pissed.

"What the fuck did you say to Ben about me?" His eyes are bloodshot and his hands are shaking. His shoulders are moving up and down fast and his fists become clenched. I know Jamie well, he's more than pissed. He might become violent. I instinctively move back.

"The truth," I say, trying to keep my voice even as I keep backing up. My fear is telling me to grab something, anything to hit him with. I've seen what Jamie can do when he's pissed.

"And what's that?" he spat.

I can't speak, my jaw is locked tight.

"Answer me!" he shouts.

"That you think Riot Radio is bullshit," I whisper, fighting back tears. He leans in and I smell the alcohol on his breath. My heart is pounding too hard. The tears are stinging my eyes. I feel myself growing smaller and smaller. I told myself no one is ever going to make me feel like that again. I gather all my anger and all the courage I have left.

"Listen, you little dip-shit, you back the fuck off me." I make myself as big as possible. He is done fucking with my head. "You are nothing but a fucking fake."

"Oh, and you're real, with your 'I'm such a fucked-up, misunderstood girl'," he says, mocking me.

"Oh, that shit's real. I'm fucking insane. You better back off," I say coldly.

"You just fucking wait." I'm shaking hard now. But not with fear. I'm fucking pissed. "Riot Radio is going to be bigger than Velvet Rage will ever be. Fuck you!" I slam my door and deadbolt the lock. I sink to the floor, shaking.

The next morning I'm at Ben's door with some super strong coffee. I knock and I'm surprised to see Ben beaming at me. No one has ever been this happy to see me, not since Jamie. Jamie. Fuck, it feels like a knife is back in my chest.

"Are you ok? he asks.

"Jamie came to see me. He wasn't too happy." I say dryly.

Ben shakes his head. "I already told him I'm not going to see him again. Not after what he said to you. He can go fuck himself. Is that coffee for me?" he asks beaming.

I could stay in his warmth all day. "Yeah. Let's go interview this kid."

"I get to interview him, too?" he asks nervously.

"Yeah ask him whatever you want—unless it's a question about his favourite fetish, then I'm out."

Ben laughs and I manage a smile.

"Uh … um … what if he's gay?"

"Benjamin, you do realize we are both gay, right?" I say with a laugh in my voice.

"Uh yeah … I mean what if I like him and he's gay?"

"He's in high school," I remind him.

"Um … so am I, but I dropped out," he mutters, looking at the concrete sidewalk.

"Then date away," I say calmly.

"Really?"

"Yeah, just don't ever fuck on my black velvet couch," I say, walking backward and pointing finger guns at him. "You'll be a dead man."

"Okay," he says, laughing.

"I'm serious, Benjamin," I say laughing with him. And for one moment I'm actually happy.

I bump into someone and I turn around to see a boy in a purple and black hoodie, tight black skinny jeans and wide green eyes.

"Uh hey, um, I'm looking for Riot Radio. Do you guys know where I can find it?" he asks.

This must the kid. I take him in more closely before I answer. He has pale skin, sandy brown hair and is wearing beat up purple converse sneakers.

I spread my arms. "You're looking at it." He steps back, his eyes widening. I watch him take us in. "I'm Sasha. That's Ben."

"Taylor," he says looking at us skeptically.

"Come in," I say with my boss lady voice.

I watch him take in the endless pile of records, radio equipment and my prized black velvet couch.

"Take a seat," I say, waving my hand towards the desk and chairs.

He takes a seat and Ben and I sit on the other side of the table. I lean back, asserting my best boss pose.

"Taylor, tell me little about yourself," I begin.

I've never fucking interviewed anyone before in my whole fucking life, but I know that's usually how they start. I'll just fake it till I do know what the fuck I'm talking about.

"Um … I love your station. I um … I like to draw and collect records." Taylor doesn't meet our gaze; his eyes are focused hard on the desk.

He collects records. One point for Taylor.

"What bands are you into?" I ask.

I watch his face light up, the way mine used to when talking about favourite bands. Now I just have a bitter, jaded 'I know more than you' look.

"I love Bowie and Arcade Fire. Uh … Death From Above 1979, The Killers, The Kills, Joy Division."

"How's your work ethic ?" Ben asks.

Point for Ben for a normal interview question.

"Uh … pretty shitty, to be honest." I watch his hands tighten. Ben and I exchange looks.

"Are you willing to sort records and go out buy them at our request?" I ask.

"Uh yeah, I'd do that," he mumbles still looking anywhere but us.

"Are you willing to work long hours?" Ben asks.

Between the two of us, we actually sound fucking professional. I wonder if he buys it?

"Uh yeah, that's fine."

"Will you get pissy if you are asked to go for coffee and food runs?" I ask, with my eyebrow raised.

Taylor leans in, tapping his fingers on the table.

"Honestly?" he asks.

"Yes, I would like an honest answer," Ben says, all formal and professional.

"Wouldn't you, Sasha?" I try to mirror Ben's professionalism. His straight back, folded hands and the natural look on his face.

"Yes, we would like that."

"I'd get pissy if I had to do it like all the time," he mutters.

Ben and I exchange looks once more. "Fair enough," I say. I have a shit work ethic and look what I've done. Fuck it … I can't send him back out there. I sigh. It will be only my fault if he fucks this up royally.

"You're in," I tell him.

Taylor breaks into a grin, his leg bouncing up and down. The tension seems to have left, but he still won't make eye contact with us.

"When do I start?" He asks.

"Right now," I say.

His smile fades. His body and face tense. "I've got somewhere I've got to be. Is that a problem?" His expression tells us he is hoping we will say 'no'. I could be a bitch and tell him to leave and not come back, but I've decided I'll only be bitch boss when I need to. Right now, I don't need to be crushing any dreams.

"No that's cool. Come tomorrow from eight a.m to one a.m."

"Sweet! Thanks so much. I won't let you down."

Taylor has an infectious grin on his face and his whole body is twitching.

"See you tomorrow, newbie," I say, grinning.

I stare into space, not moving. Something has sparked. Thoughts flowing hard and fast in my mind.

"What are your thinking about, boss lady?" Ben asks, leaning close to me to get my attention.

"We are going to make this the biggest underground operation this world has ever seen. Ben, grab my laptop."

Hours later, we have an ad for jobs on every record store site, bookstore site, and underground clothing store.

"Is this legal?" Ben asks.

"I won't tell if you won't!" My body tenses up; I won't let anything get in my way or stop me from making this the biggest underground operation this world has ever seen. For a moment I think Ben is going to bolt. I can't read his expression. But then I've never been good at reading people. My leg bounces up and down hard. I will my hands not to shake. Strength, don't fucking leave me now.

"Let's make this the biggest underground operation in the world," he says.

I break out in a grin.

"Welcome to Riot Radio, Benjamin."

The next day Taylor is late.

"Ben, did we make a mistake hiring him?" I mutter. "The asshole is late on this first day."

Ben looks at me, wide-eyed, trying to read me. The only time he's seen me vulnerable was when I broke down; the rest of the time I'm really fucking good at hiding it. Too good. It might be the death of me.

The door whips open. It's Taylor. His hair's a mess and there are dark circles under his eyes. It looks like he just threw on whatever was clean from a pile on the floor. I can't judge—I do it all the time. But he's late. I push down how pissed off I am. It's his first day, gotta cut him a bit of slack.

"Sorry, I'm late. I slept through my alarm and missed the early bus."

My jaw tightens, but I'm going to give him a chance. I'm not going to turn into a boss on a fucking power trip. "Taylor, go sort through the records. Organize them by band and genre. Ben, look through the sites and see if anyone applied for a job."

Taylor freezes. "Am I in trouble? I'm sorry… I won't be late again." His eyes are wide with panic. I hate how vulnerable he looks, like he's going to break down and I'm the one who could break him. That's not me. People break me, not the other way around.

"Look Taylor," I say. "This isn't your typical job. I'm not going to get pissed if you're late sometimes. I'm not going to be pissed if you come hungover sometimes. Just don't royally fuck up and don't fuck anyone on my couch."

"Uh, yeah … no problem," he says relieved.

"I'm going on the air." I say, "Hello, all the misfits and freaks out there who are awake or the ones who have stayed up all night. I have a proposition for all of you. Check out your local record store, bookstore or alt clothing store site. Don't come here and try to kick my ass for selling out. For one I will kick your ass, two I'm not fucking selling out. I'd rather be fucking dead," I sneer.

"Instead, we want you to check out our ad and apply to work at Riot Radio. That's right, Riot Radio is hiring. Help us make this the world's biggest underground operation. You can find us at 111 Queen Street East, Toronto. Now here is Jack White with *Icky Thump*. If all you punks get pissed, take it up with management," I sneer.

I indicate to Ben to come over. "What's up boss lady?"

"How's Taylor doing?" I say, with most of my attention figuring out what to play next.

"He's um … um … he's passed out."

I turn to see Taylor passed out on the ratty plaid couch at the other end of the room. At least he's not drooling on my black velvet couch.

"I have an idea, but you might not like it," I say looking at the passed-out Taylor.

"Fire away," Ben says.

"Can Taylor crash at your place?"

I watch Ben tilt his head. It's like I can see the gears turning in his head. I've never been able to see that with people. With Ben, it's different, like we're in sync.

"Sure," he says casually.

"Seriously?" I ask, my eyebrows raised. "You can say no, you know that right?"

"I know. But I get lonely." I didn't expect him to be so honest. Guilt churns in my stomach, it's my fault he's not with Jamie, that he's alone. I try hard to shake off the guilt; Jamie's an asshole. Ben is better off without him.

"Do you ever get lonely?" Ben asks gently.

"Sometimes." I have never been that honest with anyone before. But Ben is different. He is all warmth, caring, and honesty. With him, it doesn't feel like I'm breaking my armour when I'm honest.

"Go wake Taylor up."

I sit behind the desk like a punk godfather. Taylor is twitching everywhere, his eyes, hands, legs.

"I know … I know I'll pack my shit," Taylor says groggily.

"That's not how we work here. We find misfits, we don't throw them out. Ben has offered for you to room with him if you want."

"Where do you live?" Taylor asks as he looks up at Ben, his green eyes taking up his entire face.

"We live a few blocks from here," I say wanting control of this conversation.

"You guys live together?" he asked, surprised.

"Next to each other in the same building," I clarify.

"Are you sure?" he asks, his green eyes still wide.

"Yeah," Ben says.

"Sweet. You guys are amazing. No one has ever been this nice to me before." He looks at us like he can't trust it.

"I think we both wrote the book on that," I murmur.

We leave Riot Radio together at one in the morning. Taylor and Ben are buzzing with excitement. It's contagious.

"I can't believe I'm working and living in the city," says Taylor beaming. "I don't have to deal with asshole jocks, stupid ass classes and especially my parents." He doesn't look like I did when I moved to the city: caged, angry … fucking drunk.

It makes me feel good. I can't remember that the last time I did something nice for someone that wasn't Jamie. I feel almost protective of Taylor. If someone tries to make his smile fade, I'll break their fucking jaw.

"How did you parents react when you told them you're moving out?" Ben asks. Ben is all warmth and empathy. I was fooled when I thought Jamie was the best thing that would ever happen to me.

"Haven't told them. I will tomorrow," he said with resolution.

My anxiety makes me cringe. I'm gripped with a fear of Taylor being taken away, just when I start feeling that this will work out with him.

"Welcome to the dream," Ben says, beaming.

"And the fucking nightmare," I say.

Taylor hesitates. "Are you guys sure about this?"

"Yeah, I'm cool," Ben says.

"Welcome to the Riot Radio Family. You get family discounts," I say mockingly.

When we reach our building I say, "Night, see you guys at eight a.m. Show up on time or I'll kick your asses."

I sink into my bed and troll the sites where we placed the ads. I see a few people have applied. *Fuck you, Jamie.* I stare straight ahead, my jaw tight. *Fuck you for making me feel like nothing, like less than nothing.* Riot Radio will be the black Doc Marten that crushes *you* into nothing.

The next morning there's a tentative knock on my door. I open it in my ratty, black robe. My eyes adjust to find Sophia. There is no makeup on her face, she looks younger and more vulnerable. Her grey eyes are wide.

"Sasha I'm so sorry about what happened with Jamie, but I really need him as a bassist for my band."

Sadness and anger well up in my chest, pushing each other, making my rib cage rattle. Anger boils hot and I let it win.

"I don't fucking have time for this," I snarl.

"Sasha, please. At least until I find someone to replace him," she pleads. "I'm sorry he hurt you."

Tears form in my eyes. I want to say it's okay, that I understand, but I told myself I wasn't going to let anyone walk all over me again.

"I have a fucking radio station to run," I spit.

Ben and Taylor come out of Ben's apartment.

"Come in, gentlemen," I say, leaving Sophia standing in the hallway with her mouth wide open and her eyes welling with tears.

CHAPTER 15

I'VE NEVER SEEN SO MANY FREAKS AND GEEKS IN ONE PLACE

"HOLY shit is this for us? I ask.

There is a line of people decked out in plaid and black leather. It's an endless line of mohawks and fading, dyed hair. A sea of swirling tattoos and glinting silver piercings. All in front of Riot Radio.

I strut over with all the power I can command in my little body.

"Who's here for Riot Radio?" I say as loud as humanly possible. Everyone turns their head. *Holy Shit. Holy Fuck.* "We will be with you all in ten!"

I usher Ben and Taylor inside. "Put three sets of desks and chairs together."

"Three?" Ben asks.

"Plans have changed. Taylor, you will be conducting interviews."

"Are you sure?" Ben asks, his eyes wide. "I mean, you're the boss, but are you sure?"

I swallow my 'I'm fucking sure' response and say, "I can't risk anyone leaving cuz they got bored."

"But it's my second day!" Taylor protests.

"Just get the desks together and I'll write up some basic questions," I say, "Then ask them about music and shit, okay?"

"Okay," Ben says.

"Yes, ma'am," Taylor replies. I smirk. Ma'am. I like it.

I grab a blank piece of paper and a pen and frantically scrawl the questions down.

Tell me a bit about yourself.

I remember what Ben asked, and write:

What is your work ethic like?

Then I write:

What music do you like?

Oh, and:

Do you have radio station experience?

Can you work long hours?

And finally, the ground rules:

Show up on time, don't be hungover and don't fuck on my black velvet couch!

Okay good. "Get ready gentlemen, this is war," I say. Then I open the door to all the tired, worn and expectant faces.

"Interviews have now begun!" I shout, "Three at a time! Sit at a desk and let us know your name."

People are rushing in, trying to be first. My anxiety grows, trying to eat away at my confidence. Maybe I should I have hired someone for crowd control!

> Images of screaming girls, fighting with all their strength in the muscled arms of policemen. Glass shattering ... Sonia, in the arms of someone else.

I break through the memory, it feels like coming to the surface in ice cold water.

The first guy to sit with me has a cocky grin on his face. I don't like him already.

"I'm Derek."

"Tell me a little bit about yourself, Derek."

He leans back, still cocky as fuck. "I used to work at my dad's record store so I know all about vinyl…how to play them, the difference between a 33 and 45, how to tell the quality of a record, how rare it is and where it's been imported from."

"That's pretty impressive," I admit even though I still don't like him. "What's your work ethic?"

"If I find something interesting, I'll do it."

"What kind of music you interested in?"

"Punk, alt stuff."

"You ever worked at a radio station before?"

He puts his lips together. "Nope."

"You willing to work long hours?"

"Yeah, got nothing else to do." He shrugs.

I take him in, he has a cocky grin with dark brown hair slicked back. It's a bit greasy and his eyes are brown, matching his hair. He's wearing a worn leather jacket that is too big for him.

"Okay, some ground rules. If you get this job, don't come late or hungover every day. You can't get pissy if someone asks you to grab coffee or food for everyone. You gotta be cool sorting through records and buying them with company money. I don't give a fuck if you bring a friend or whatever, but they better not break anything and if I'm not here, don't fuck on my velvet couch."

"Can I fuck on it if you *are* here?"

I want to punch that fucking grin off his smug face. Instead I say, "Got it?"

"Yeah." I can tell he's not used to people standing up to him.

"Leave your name, number and email. We'll get back to you in two days if you got the job."

"Okay. I can handle that." He scribbles his info and walks out, winking at me as he leaves. If he thinks he can get this job just by looks he can fucking forget it. I'm gay as fuck.

"Hey, I'm Talia." I look up at this girl with short, lavender-coloured hair. She has a big, silver nose ring and a leather choker. She's wearing a velvet, black tank, black leather jacket, ripped fishnets and worn black Docs. She has these huge, greenish-blue eyes that run shivers down my spine.

"Tell me about yourself, Talia," I say folding my hands tightly.

"I worked at an underground radio station, but they turned mainstream so I quit," she sneers, her face twisting in disgust. "I work at a punk record store right now. I saw your ad on our site. Not exactly legal, huh?"

The way she says it is like that doesn't matter at all. I smirk.

"What music do you like?" I ask.

"Punk, some alt-goth stuff."

"How's your work ethic?"

"I get shit done."

"You cool working long hours?"

"Whatever."

"Ground rules …"

"Let me guess … don't be chronically late or chronically hungover, don't break shit, do coffee runs and record runs and no fucking on the job."

"Yeah, that's basically it. How do you know the ground rules?"

"I've worked in places like this before. Like I said underground shit."

"Okay …"

"Leave my name, number, and email. Yeah, I've done this before," she says knowingly.

"We'll call in two days if you get it." I tell her even though I want her to start right away.

"Cool." She rewards me a smile as she leaves that makes my body tense. A feeling of dread creeps through me. Why did she make feel like this? It's like she brings destruction with her. Usually, I fucking love that … but today something is wrong.

I shake the thoughts from my brain and move on to the next person in line.

At the end of the day, we are sprawled on the floor of Riot Radio surrounded by papers with notes scrawled on them and greasy hamburger wrappers.

"Okay, we are going to tell each other the two people we liked best. I'll go first."

The image of Talia and her lavender hair forms in my mind. She was the most qualified but there is something else … something tugging at the back of my mind that I can't understand.

"There was Talia who worked at a radio station before and now works at a punk record store. She is very qualified," I say.

Ben and Taylor turn to look at each other.

"What?" I ask trying to figure out that look.

"Is that the only reason?" Taylor asks playfully.

"Uh … yeah," I say.

Ben tilts his head and smiles. "Don't make me get it out of you," he says.

"How would you do that?" I counter.

Before I see it coming I'm being attacked with greasy hamburger wrappers.

"Okay, okay," I say with my hands up. "I give in." I can't help but laugh. "She is cute."

"I knew it!" Taylor said triumphantly, a grin splitting his face.

"Speaking of cute," Ben says.

"Yes, Benjamin?" I ask.

"What about that guy with the greaser look?"

"Oh … Derek?"

"Yeah, he knew a lot about vinyl. Yeah, I'd consider him. He's cute I guess? I can't fucking tell with men. You guys all look like stick figures to me," I say.

"I look like a stick figure to you?" Ben asks.

I ignore his question.

"Well, he's cute," Ben says.

"I second that." We both turn to look at Taylor. "

I never thought I would be here. At my own radio station surrounded by people who accept me. Respect me. Me, Sasha. The girl who would never amount to anything. I struggle to push the images of Melanie's father screaming, his pudgy face almost purple telling me how disgusting I am.

"Ben, who did you think could work here?" I ask as I struggle to surface above the memories.

By the end, we narrow it down to Talia, Derek, a tall punk with an even taller blonde mohawk, a femme boy and a trans girl.

"Who are we hiring?" Taylor asks.

I picture each person milling around doing their jobs. Then I see more; I see us building Riot Radio into the biggest underground venture this world has ever seen.

"All of them," I say.

A few days later we are preparing ourselves for all the new people we hired. Taylor just came back from a coffee run and even remembered to get milk and sugar for their drinks. I want to show the new hires that even though I'll be a tough bitch when I need to be, I give a fuck about them. That's why I also bought toasted bagels—if they are as fucking poor as I was, at least they'll have breakfast.

"They're here!" Taylor shouted, looking out the iron door.

"Send them in," I say, feeling like I'm a general who just called her troops to battle.

Taylor opens the door and they mill in.

"You're all here because you got the job," I say.

"Fuck, yeah," Talia says. Everyone else just stands there looking surprised.

"I got coffee and bagels for everyone. Grab your food and I'm going to tell you what you are going to do."

I'm really fucking short. I'm trying to stand up as tall as possible; that way they'll take me seriously. They gather around me, still making me feel like a fucking general.

"Who's good with computers?" I ask.

"That's me," says Cassandra. She's trans, tall with long, thick, brown hair, winged eyeliner and sliver piercings. She's covered in intricate tattoos. She's wearing a short leather skirt and fishnets, with high black heels.

"You will be in charge of making a website where people can play our station. Derek, you're good with records, you'll buy the records we need. Talia you will help me with the radio side. Who's good at decorating?"

"Stereotypically, I am," Timothy, the femme boy, says. Like Cassandra, he also has winged eyeliner as well as thick, shiny, purple eyeshadow; a black, velvet sweater; a short, black, leather shirt; and, shiny black Docs.

"You are going to redesign Riot Radio's headquarters. Work it around the black, velvet couch."

"Good. Right now it looks like a dump," he says, scrunching his nose in disgust.

"Steven," I point to the tall, blonde punk. "You are sorting records and doing coffee and food runs." Steven just nods.

"Taylor and Ben, you will manage everyone."

Pleased with the new team, I pause to watch Timothy hang up a poster of Sid and Nancy. As Derek grabs some cash to buy more records, Steven sorts records and Talia comes to help me set up to go on the air. At that moment I think we'll fucking make it.

With Talia's help, I'm quickly on the air. "Thanks to all the outcasts that came for the interviews. If you weren't picked, well that's not my fucking problem."

Talia leans in. "Tell them you're playing *Bang Bang* by Green Day."

"What?" I mouth.

"Trust me," she mouths back.

"We are going to play *Bang Bang* by Green Day," I announce.

I play it and lean back. It has that punk beat I like, but something doesn't feel right. It's making my chest tight and my stomach churn. Is it Talia? I look at her out of the corner of my eye. Her wing-tipped eyes are going over the controls. It's like everything in me is screaming to run or fight. I can't fucking fire her based on a feeling. I'll tell Ben to keep an eye on her. Keep your enemies close, right?

The panel lights up. "You're on Riot Radio."

"That song was great! I can't believe that was Green Day!"

"They can surprise you," I say.

"Pretty good for a bunch of faggots."

The blood freezes in my veins. Everyone turns to look at me. Waiting to see how I'm going to react. Waiting to see if their new boss is a homophobic bitch. The answer for me is easy.

"Get that word off my fucking station, you dick," I snarl. I don't want to turn around, but I have to. I need to know their reaction to how I handled it.

Cassandra and Tim are grinning. Taylor is giving me a small smile and Ben is nodding his head in approval. I can't read Talia's expression. After work, I tell Talia to stay behind.

"Am I in trouble?" she asked incredulously even though I sense she wants to say, "What the fuck do you want?" I can see the rage pulsing through her veins. I can tell because that's how I look when I'm fucking pissed off.

"No, not all. I just want to make sure you're cool with queer people."

"Yeah, I'm cool."

"Okay."

"Is that all?" she demands.

"Yeah." As she walks away, my stomach sinks. Something is wrong.

CHAPTER 16

DO YOU LIKE THE TALKING HEADS?

"**THIS** album is shit!"

"It isn't fucking shit!"

"We aren't playing that!"

I come into work and see Derek looking like Bender from *The Breakfast Club* and Taylor in his signature purple hoodie, both leaning in, looking predatory. Derek has a black album in his hand.

I tense up. I fucking hate fighting. I've been in way too many fights for one lifetime. Ben rushes past me, blue eyes wide.

"Guys, fucking break it up," he hisses.

Ben looks at me frantically, like he'll get in trouble as a manager because I'm walking into a fight he isn't controlling. Taylor shakes his head hard, sandy blonde hair flying in every direction. He points his finger at Derek, his face red with anger. His shoulders shaking hard.

"He bought shit with company money! He should know better than to buy this shit!"

"Okay, what is this shit you're talking about?" I ask calmly.

"Here boss, tell them it isn't shit!" Derek says, thrusting the album at me.

I take it and examine it. It says Talking Heads, *Fear of Music*.

"Talking Heads isn't shit," I murmur.

"This one is!" Taylor snarls.

I take a closer look at the songs on the back. I see *Life During Wartime* on the back.

"We can play *Life During Wartime*," I say. Derek grins triumphantly.

"Next time, never buy a record for one song," I add. I watch Derek's face fall from a cocky grin to smirk. Taylor stares stonily at him.

"Come with me," I say to Derek and Taylor, motioning to the back where Timothy is sketching out designs. "Timothy, can you give us a second?"

"Sure thing, boss lady," he says and sashays away.

"Okay, guys I have a fucking radio station to run. What the fuck is going on?" I say, stone-cold calm.

"I just don't want him buying *shit*," Taylor mutters.

Derek snarls. "I don't buy shit!"

"Okay Taylor, how about you take on the role of field manager?"

"What's that?" I see Taylor's face light up. He's not used to people believing in him. None of us are. "You are going hang out with Derek while he looks for records. You'll give him advice on what we're looking for. When you feel everything is cool, Derek can go on his own."

"You're fucking giving me a babysitter?" Derek spits at me. He is practically shaking, he's so pissed off. That macho shit doesn't scare me.

"You want this fucking job or not ?" I fire back.

"Fuck fine, whatever."

"Hey Sasha, can I talk to you after the shift is over?" Taylor whispers.

"Yeah of course," I whisper back.

"No more fucking fighting, guys," I say, louder.

I go over and see if Talia has everything set to go on the air and see that she is in my spot.

"I was thinking I could go on the air today," she says.

Why does it feel like the world is being taken out from under me? "Um how about I show you a few more times, just so you can see how we do things here?"

"Yeah, of course," she says as she moves over reluctantly.

I click the button and we are on the air. "I can see we have some people waiting to call in. Misfits of this fucked-up world, Riot Radio is getting a website. We are joining this decade ... well kind of. But not totally, because this decade fucking sucks. No one knows what a 45 is anymore. Fuck I sound like my grandma. Let's see what you weirdos have to say."

The calls come in:

"Do you really have a drag queen working for you?"

"Is Riot Radio a bunch of queers?"

"I think I saw a fairy come in the other day."

I lean in, rage sparking something inside me.

"Listen, if you ever call into this station again I will find out where you live and I will get into your head so badly they will have to take you away in a straight jacket."

"Are you threatening me?"

"Fuck, yes." I turn to see everyone stopped to look at me. "I don't take shit," I say.

"Impressive," Derek says.

"I like her already," Cassandra said grinning. Ben looks uneasy, I don't catch his eye. This is me, take it or get the fuck out.

After the shift, Taylor is standing awkwardly in front of my desk. "What's going on?" I ask. I wait while he shuffles his feet. His eyes are glued to the floor.

"I can't work next Wednesday. I know I just started, but I can't miss this."

"What's going on?" I ask.

"Promise you won't tell anyone?" He whispers, eyes pleading.

"Only if you won't tell anyone that I had a crush on Katy Perry."

"I won't because that's really embarrassing," he says, laughing.

"Thank you." I laugh, too. "What's up?"

"I … I … need to go start hormones."

I tilt my head. Is he passing really well as a guy, or is that a girl underneath that hoodie?

"I … um … I'm female to male. I could tell that's what you were wondering," he says, swallowing hard. "I'm going to get my first shot."

"Do you want me to come with you?" I whisper. That protectiveness is there again. I don't want him doing something that fucking major alone.

"That's really nice of you." I can tell by his face that he really means it. "I was thinking of asking Ben?"

"Yeah, I can handle a day without you two."

"I know you can," he says, grinning.

The next day I notice Ben and Taylor's absence more than I thought I would. I guess I got used to Ben's warmth and Taylor's protective attitude toward the company. Taylor's like me, he doesn't take shit.

I hate that it came to this for all of us. Having to leave home because we are fucking different. Because people labeled us freaks in the worst way. That's why I don't take anyone's shit. I'm done with people walking all over me because I'm not like them. Fuck that shit.

"Sasha?" I am pulled back to reality by Cassandra leaning over me, her thick, velvety voice in my ear.

"What's up?"

"The website is done. Tell me what you think."

I look over to the laptop she's holding. 'Riot Radio' is written in bold black letters like it's from an old-school typewriter. There's a collage of rock stars and punks in black and white in the background. I see Sid and Nancy, Joey Strummer, Joan Jett, Cherie Currie, The Ramones and many other kickass musicians.

"There's a place where you can post comments, listen to old broadcasts and listen live online," Cassandra explains.

"This is fucking amazing," I let out a long breath.

"Can I talk to you privately for a minute?" she asks, her eyes narrowing a little.

"Yeah of course."

We step outside into the cool, fall air. I watch her light a cigarette and take a slow drag. "You smoke?" she asks. "Or I am corrupting an innocent, young girl?"

I laugh and shake my head hard. "It's too late for that." She laughs too, deep and throaty probably from years of smoking.

"I heard you talking to Taylor and I need a day off, too." Is everyone just going to ask for time off and will I be too nice to say 'no' every fucking time?

"That expression on your face is why I wanted to talk privately. I don't want everyone taking advantage of how much you care about us."

They can tell I care? I don't know if I like that or not. I don't like people seeing the vulnerability under my armour. I've been hurt too many fucking times for that.

"I heard Taylor say he needs to go for hormones and … I need to go, too."

"Take a few days. No problem," I say.

"Oh honey, I won't be gone more than a day. This isn't my first time. But you might want to figure out a set number of days we can take off at a time."

I nod. I watch her eyes trace my face.

"What's going on, hon?"

"Something doesn't feel right." I look away into the grey sky and the thick, looming clouds.

"Are you sick, honey?" she asks, leaning in, searching me more intently now.

"No … like … something's coming. I know it sounds stupid but I think it has something to do with Talia."

"It's not stupid when it's your intuition, hon," she murmurs. "I'll keep an eye on Talia for you." Her voice low and protective. "I'll be gone Monday. Okay, hon?"

"No problem."

"Now excuse me, I have a goth bitch to watch," she says sauntering into the store.

The next morning, I came in to find Derek sneering, "Where were you and Ben yesterday, Taylor?"

"None of your fucking business."

"Was he fucking your business?" he laughed.

"Derek, the fuck?" I say.

"Oh, hey boss lady." He says, giving me a sleazy smile.

"Don't think I won't fucking fire you, Taylor could do your job easy," I snarl.

He holds his hands up in surrender. "I'll be good!" he says, with that same fucking grin.

I shake my head. I'm about to sit when Talia comes over.

"I brought some records from home I thought we could play."

"Okay, let's take a look."

We go over to our broadcast station and she sets them down. The first one I recognize, The Cramps, the others I have no idea who they are.

"I was reading on the website that people wanted more goth stuff," Talia said.

"Really?" I say. "Most of the listeners are into punk and indie."

She shrugs.

"We can give it a try, just not right now," I say.

I watch Talia's body tense and I see her struggle to keep her face even.

"I wanna talk about what to do with all this queer bashing in the comments," I say.

"Besides threatening that you will put them in a straight jacket?" she says, arching a black eyebrow.

"Yeah, I have only so many of those comments."

"I doubt it," said Talia smiling. I made this pissed-off, alt, goth girl smile. But for the first time, there is nothing in me that's happy that I caused someone to truly smile. I put that thought in the back of my mind for later.

"Um, I was wondering if you wanna grab a drink later," she asks. "You're into girls, right?"

How the fuck did she know I'm gay? It's not like I hide it, but I don't fucking broadcast it either. She looks at me expectantly from under black, wing-tipped eyelids.

"I don't think …" Fuck it. This isn't an office. I can go out for a drink. "Yeah, I'd like that." I push down the bad feeling I get around her. Maybe it will help if I get to know her better.

I'm rewarded with another smile, this one wider, tugging her black-painted lips.

"Gather around, everyone!" I shout.

I watch Cassandra look up from her laptop, Timothy from his fabrics and everyone else from the records. I wait and everyone comes toward me and Talia.

"Okay, we know there's been a lot of queer-bashing lately. What the fuck are we going to do about it?" I ask. "I want to hear your suggestions."

"Hunt them down so we can beat the shit out of them," Cassandra snarls.

"I like that a lot," I say, grinning. "But how about something that won't get us thrown in jail."

"I have an idea." We all turn to look at Ben who is in the back, wearing a denim shirt with his sleeves rolled-up.

"Let's hear it, Ben," I say.

"We can have a moderator for the online bashing."

"I think Cassandra should do it."

She smiles huge, revealing broken teeth. "Gladly hon."

"What about on the air?" I ask.

"Just cut them off," Timothy says. "Show them it won't be tolerated, without treating them badly."

"Good ideas," I say. "Anyone else?"

I notice Talia shift away. That feeling is coming back. That feeling that something is off. Something with Talia is definitely off. Looks like tonight I'm going to be in bed with the enemy.

I walk into the punk club Talia wants to meet in. There's already a band onstage, and people violently moshing in the pit. I see her at the end of the bar. It's covered in black, chipping paint and peeling band stickers. I push past punks that smell of beer, sweat and old leather. They snarl at me, but I don't give a fuck.

I sit next to her and she's smiling. Fucking smiling. Talia never smiles. Never.

"Why do you never smile at work?" I ask her.

She laughs, her greenish-blue eyes dancing and her painted, black lips curling up.

"Fuck, your boss must be terrible then." I laugh, leaning back, letting the tension leave my shoulders.

"The worst, but she's kind of hot so …" she said, raising her dyed, black eyebrows. That smile is still there.

"Oh yeah?" I say, grinning.

"Yeah, she's a bit of a badass too."

I haven't felt like this, not since Sonia. That feeling that maybe you're not as worthless as you think.

"What are you drinking?" I yell. "I need a fucking drink."

"Just a beer. I'll get you one," she offers.

I down it fast, not thinking that I shouldn't be doing this … again. I just need my mind to be quiet.

Talia laughs and puts her hand on my knee. She leans in close and whispers, "Kiss me."

My head is hazy and everything feels so warm and so fucking wrong all at the same time. I lean towards her because I want to forget. This is part of the addiction for me, the kissing, the fucking. Getting beat up at the end. Doing it all over again. I thought I was better than this now. I guess I was fucking wrong. I can feel something on my tongue and I take it, no questions asked. I feel so hazy. I let it take over until everything is blurry and this calm comes over me. I feel her taking my hand and I let her lead me to the mosh pit. I smile at the crush of bodies, the sweat, the haze. *I Wanna Be Your Dog* blasting through the speakers.

CHAPTER 17

WHAT THE FUCK DID YOU DO, SASHA? NIGHT ME IS A DUMBASS

THE next morning, I wake up with a pulsing headache. I can barely see. The worst thing is that my hands are shaking. My body needs a drink. I told myself shit like this isn't going to happen. It can't happen. Not again. I have a fucking radio station to run. Not just any station. Riot fucking Radio. Where freaks find peace in a world that wants to chew them up and spit them out. I cover my face with my hands, ignoring the shaking in them. I get up and throw on some sweats. I need a fucking coffee and something greasy. I stagger to the coffee shop a few blocks down. The one I always go to after I fall off the wagon and get fucked up again. I get my usual hangover meal - black coffee, and a greasy grilled cheese sandwich. I'm about to leave when I feel there is someone looking at me. I spin around hard and see Jamie. I start to walk the other way, but he grabs my arm.

"Let go or I'll scream," I spit. He lets go, but my arm burns where he touched it.

"You fell off the wagon." It wasn't a question.

"Why the fuck do you care?" I snarl.

"You called me worthless and showed up at my apartment fucking drunk and treating me like I'm shit. What did you expect would happen?"

He just stares at me like he can see right through me. I hate when he does that.

"Sophia misses you," he says.

"What about Jamie? Does he miss me?" I demand.

He shakes his head. "You weren't good for me. You're just a kid."

"You're a fucking snake, Jamie. Excuse me, I have a radio station to run."

I get there early and see Ben sipping coffee and going through records. He looks up, wide-eyed, when he sees me.

"Hey, you okay?" he asks.

When I don't say anything he comes over and wraps his arms around me. He smells like coffee and cinnamon. What did I do to deserve Ben?

"No," I sob, "I'm not. I fell off the wagon. I drank, got high," I whisper.

"What? What happened?"

I try not to get lost in the deep blue of Ben's eyes. "I went on a date. We drank and got stoned. I'm not proud of it, I'm not fucking proud of it." The hot tears are coming down again. I start to shake in Ben's arms. I need his warmth now more than ever. "Then … I … I fucking saw Jamie at my favourite hangover cafe. He made me feel like shit again. I don't know how he ever made me happy." I let the fat tears roll down my face landing in my mouth, tasting like salt.

"I have an idea," Ben murmured into my shoulder.

"What?" I ask softly. Ben just smiles slowly and goes to the record player.

American Idiot by Green Day blasts through the speakers. Ben takes my hands and leads me to the couch.

"Can I have this dance?"

"Sure, why the fuck not," I say.

Ben laughs. "So dignified," he says. His deep blue eyes light up.

"You should know what you are getting into when you ask someone to dance," I laugh.

"So true," he smiles.

We jump up and down on the couch screaming, "*I don't wanna be an American idiot!*" at the top of our lungs. For the first time in a long time, I really smile. I really fucking smile.

We stop when we hear the door open. It's Taylor looking at us, surprised by the scene. "Did I miss the memo? Early meeting that includes jumping on couches?" he asks.

"Fuck yeah, you did." I laugh.

Taylor shrugs, comes to join us and screams over the music. "I'm getting top surgery!"

For a moment no one moves, then we hug each other tightly while jumping on the couch. We're having a real fucking movie moment before everything goes to shit. As *American Idiot* ends, we jump off the couch just as the others arrive.

Talia is hovering near my chair right before I go on air, her eyes searching my face.

"Did you get a chance to look at the records I brought in?" She asks.

"Uh yeah, I did. We can't play those." For a moment I see something in Talia's eyes, something dark that makes my stomach knot.

"Why not?" she questions. Her face settles into a look of pure annoyance.

"Most of our listeners are indie kids who don't mind punk and punks that don't mind indie," I say. "I searched the site and no one says they want goth. You must have read it wrong." What I'm really thinking is, *something is wrong here ... with you.* It's like a warning pulse in my veins. Pure dread.

"Okay yeah, I must have." she says dismissively.

"Get Cassandra to show you how to work the website when she gets back."

"Where did she go anyways?"

"Had a doctor's appointment," I say writing down shit to say on the air, only half paying attention.

"Couldn't she take one before or after work?"

"She made it before she started here," I say, still not giving my full attention to her.

"Well, she should have changed it."

I spin around hard, my hands shaking violently. I try hard to still them. "Listen, Talia, you aren't in charge here … I am," I say, my words and body tense. "Maybe you think that because you work up here with me, you are above everyone else. You're not," I tell her.

"Ben, Taylor and I are in charge. I fucking hate reminding people of that, so fucking do your job and only make suggestions about the tech or the music. That's fucking it."

"I'm sorry, I won't do it again," she mutters as she starts to walk away.

"Wait," I whisper. She turns around and I take her hands. "I'm sorry. Let's go out tonight."

"Okay," she nods.

I'm sleeping with the fucking enemy again!

"Okay, we're going on the air." I push the button and start.

"We're on the air, freaks, and here's a little lesson. If some asshole grabs your arm, fucking scream. Better yet, turn around and kick him the fucking nuts. No one should have to fucking deal with that shit. Girls, guys and everyone in between and outside … We are fucking better than that. Even though everyone else tells us we are shit and that we're freaks and we don't deserve to be happy, we are better than that. But we fucking do, we deserve happiness. Here's *Go Home* by Joan Jett. She wrote this with our other queen, Kathleen Hanna. It's from 1994 on her album, *Pure and Simple*. It's about some asshole following her home. She wrote this after Mia Zapata got raped and killed in an alleyway. Stay safe everyone."

I notice that everyone tears up, but because of our fucked up lives we don't want anyone to see.

Later, I'm at a bar with Talia and she leans in with a smile on those perfect, black, painted lips. "What do you want to drink?" she asks.

Thoughts are racing through my mind. I know if I have even one drink, it's going to lead to me drinking till I'm off my face drunk. Then when I'm off my face drunk, I'll get high. Other thoughts tell me to relax, it's only one drink. But I know myself, it's never just one drink.

"I'll just grab a coke." I say.

Talia's eyes narrow. "You're no fun," she sneers.

There it is again, in the back of my mind, that warning to run as far away from Talia as possible.

"Well, I'm going to get drunk as fuck and we are going to … fuck." she announces.

I know this story well. I fuck, I fuck and I fuck until I get myself in a dangerous situation and I get the shit beaten out of me. But it's only Talia. It's not a hookup. If I fuck over and over it will be with her, and I'm gone.

My back slams against the bathroom stall. I haven't felt that pain in a long time. There it is, that pill on my tongue. It's just getting high … it's not drinking. I take it and smile, letting it take me away.

"Sasha what are you doing?" I hear someone say.

"Melanie?" Her blue eyes take me in. That beautiful blonde hair that I used to be jealous of is dangling all the way down her back to her hips. Her pale pink lips are pursed.

"Why are you doing this to yourself?" she asks. "What happened to you?" Her eyes fill with tears.

It feels like someone has grabbed me and violently shaken me awake. I'm covered in cold sweat, my body shaking. It was only a dream. It was only a dream.

CHAPTER 18

IT'S CALLED SPIRALLING

I crack open my eyes and scan my apartment, but there's no one here. I'm alone.

What happened to you? That thought rolls through my mind. What happened to me?

I manage to get up and stagger to the mirror in the bathroom. My face is gaunt from not eating. My eyes are bloodshot and there are dark circles under them. My shoulder blades stick out. I'm almost nothing. It's like I'm barely here. With shaking hands I cover the bags under my eyes with foundation. I need to eat … something. I go to my mini-fridge and pull out a cold breakfast burrito. I sit cross-legged on the floor and take a huge bite. My stomach churns and I rush to the bathroom. Bile comes out as I heave into the toilet. My whole body is shaking. I sit on the cold tile and wipe my mouth. What's happening to me? I swore to myself that I would never do this again.

If I go down, Riot Radio goes down. I'd rather fucking die than see it go under because I fucked it up. I lean over the counter and brush my teeth violently until the taste of vomit leaves my mouth. I step into the shower, letting the hot water run down my body. When I step out, I go in search of clean clothes. I put on a Sex Pistols tank, black skinny jeans and a black leather jacket. I go to the mirror and outline my eyes in thick black eyeliner and put on black lipstick. I force myself to eat a piece of toast and go grab a coffee. Then I head over Riot Radio.

"I have an idea," I announce as I push open the door. Everyone turns to look at me. "Fucking staff meeting."

They all gather around me. "We're going to have local punk and indie bands play a set once a week. Cassandra, Talia and I will audition the punks. Ben and Taylor will audition the indie kids. Timothy and Steven, you will set up the station."

"What the fuck will I do?" Says Derek with his arms crossed, leaning on the back wall. I'm getting really tired of his shit.

"You're making sure no one fucks anything up."

"I'm babysitting," he sneers.

"If you don't like it you can get the fuck out."

"I fucking will," he shouts as he walks over to the door and slams it behind him.

I try not to flinch. I'm done taking shit from macho assholes. No one is going to step all over me again and if anyone messes with Riot Radio again, they're fucking dead.

"Forget him girl," Cassandra snarls. "He doesn't know how good he's got it."

"Already forgotten." I hold my head high. New Sasha is fucking queen bitch.

"Steven and Timothy keep setting up the place. I'm going on the fucking air and Talia you are going to join me." Keep your friends close and your enemies closer.

I lean forward in my chair and go on the air. "Hey, you freaks and geeks. I gotta proposition for you and it goes something like this. For all those who don't know, I referenced the show *Freaks and Geeks* and our queen Kathleen Hanna in the same fucking breath. We actually do have a proposition for you. For all the punk and indie bands we ..."

I motion to Talia to speak.

"We want you to do a set on Riot Radio, so if you have a band or just a set of fucking balls, call in or fucking show up at 111 Queen Street East," she says easily.

"Let's hear what you have to say," I say, leaning back in.

"Hey, girl."

"Hey, who's this?"

"Kathie, and I have a Riot Grrrl band. We love your station and how Joan Jett and Kathleen Hanna are your queens."

"They should be everyone's queens," I say.

She laughs. "When're the auditions?"

"Tomorrow at twelve," Talia mouths.

"Say it," I mouth back.

"It's going to be tomorrow at twelve." Talia says.

"Who's this?" asks Kathie.

"That's my new co-host," I say.

"Cool. We'll be there."

"You're on Riot Radio. Speak."

"We are a fucking professional band. We've had, like, ten gigs this month and wanna play at Riot Radio."

"Gotta audition like everyone else," Talia says.

"C'mon, don't be a bitch."

I lean in. "My station, so we can be as big a bitch as we want."

"Let's see who our next victim is."

"Hey." A nervous voice comes on the air.

"Hey, what's up?" I say.

"I ... We have a ... queer band. We ... we ... would like to play an LGBTQ safe show at your station. I don't think you guys are homophobes or anything but I wanted ... I wanted to make sure it's cool with you that we ... we are a queer band."

"Can I fucking tell you something?"

"Uh ... yeah ... yeah of course." I say.

"We are all fucking queer, except Steven."

"Nah … I'm polysexual." That is the most I have heard Steven talk.

"Never mind we are all queer." I say.

"Okay … uh … sweet. The audition is tomorrow at twelve, right?"

"Yeah show up at 111 Queen Street East. Ask for Sasha. That's me by the way."

"Oh ... oh my God ... ok … cool."

"Cool … next."

After the day is almost done, Cassandra comes up to me wielding her laptop. "Boss girl, check this out," she says with a crooked grin. I lean over to look at the website page. "Holy shit!We have a hundred auditions."

"Holy fuck! Team meeting before we go!" Everyone gathers around me. I still can't get used to that.

"Cassandra, our fucking amazing tech woman," she smiles at the word woman, "has brought to my attention that we have a hundred fucking auditions tomorrow!"

"We will open the doors right at twelve. Timothy has created two areas for the bands and has soundproofed them. We can hear two bands at once. Each band can play for one song, ideally in two minutes - three, tops. Steven, if they get pissy, or even violent, kick their asses to the curb."

"I can handle that too," Cassandra says.

"Great."

"Get their band name, style, how many people are in the band and their contact info … phone number, and address. Okay, fucking go home and rest up. Big day tomorrow kids. Big day."

CHAPTER 19

HOW MANY PUNKS FIT INTO ONE RADIO STATION? I DON'T FUCKING KNOW. YOU DO THE MATH

peel my eyes open to the mess of my apartment. I'm not ready to deal with entitled, pissy asses today who think they are the next Clash or the next fucking Beatles.

There's a knock on the door that makes me jump. I stumble to it, not bothering to make myself presentable to the outside world. I open the door to Ben, smiling and holding two cups of coffee in one hand and a paper bag in the other. "I brought you coffee and your favourite chocolate chip and banana muffin."

"Come, sit," I say, sleep still clinging to my words.

Ben sits on the bed and passes me the coffee and the muffin. "Two milks, one sugar," he says, smiling.

"Ben, what did I do to deserve you?" I ask.

"You became my friend and then offered me a cool job helping you chase your dream. I appreciate it," he says, giving me one of his warm smiles.

"Don't fucking make me cry," I say, holding in tears. I can't believe I'm showing Ben my vulnerable side again, but I know I can fucking trust him. I doubt that under all the warmth is a liar. "Let me get ready and prepare for the apocalypse," I sniff.

I'm ready in a few minutes; black skinny jeans, a black leather jacket, heavy eyeliner eyes, black lips and a white tee that says *Boss Lady* in black.

"Ben are we fucking nuts?" I ask, still looking in the mirror.

"I think so," he says, smiling.

At the station, we all hover near the door looking at all the punks and indie kids with their instruments. We came in early to set up two drum kits as well as wires, amps, and microphones. When we're done, I take a deep breath. "Fucking send them in." I mutter.

We all take our seats and Cassandra opens the door. I watch her police everyone into a line and make sure no one tramples each other to be first in through the door.

The first band is an all-girl band. The lead singer keeps eyeing me while they set up their stuff. She's got choppy hair, tight red pants, black pointed boots, a black leather belt slung over her hips and a worn black leather jacket. She struts over and holds her hand out. "I'm Kathie, we spoke on the air."

"Sasha," I say taking her hand. Who at our age fucking shakes hands?

"We're the Riot Grrrl band, we've been influenced by our queens. I think you'll like us," she says, giving me a confident grin.

"Let's hear it," I say trying not to let my interest show.

The drummer taps her sticks. "One, two, three, four!" she calls out.

Kathie swings her hips and snarls out.

> *I wanna drown all the noise out of my mind*
> *It's already too loud*
> *It roars telling me to rip skin off bone*
> *I thrash around like a wild animal in my head*
> *Why do I have to see this?*
> *Stick thin starving girls*
> *The holy ideal pics on Instagram*
> *Before and after again, again, again."*

"Stop." The band suddenly becomes still, their eyes burning into me.

"I loved it! Cassandra? Talia?"

"I hate those before and after pics on Instagram, it's like I don't need to see this. I want to go online to block that shit out. And, ya, you guys are really good," Cassandra adds.

"Talia?"

"You guys were really good, we'll definitely call you." she says.

I wince. I should be giving the last word, but I don't mention it.

"Hey." I look to see a nervous boy in front of the mic. He's skinny with curly, light-brown hair and brown eyes. He's wearing burgundy, corduroy pants and a denim shirt with a red and brown scarf tied around his neck.

"We are... a... the ... the queer band, like I mentioned. I'm David." He shakes each of our hands, his palm is sweaty. Not again with the handshakes. I resist the urge to wipe my hand on my pants.

"Nice to meet you, David," I say. Pulling out all the polite stops.

The band gets ready for their set. The guitarist has platinum-blonde hair and painted black nails. The bassist is a trans girl and I think the drummer is a trans guy.

David goes up to the mic, "We're Queer Core," he mumbles.

A punk beat starts up with an indie guitar lick accompanying it. David opens his mouth to sing, and nothing comes out.

"Um ... can ... we try again?" He asks, eyeing me desperately.

"Yeah go ahead."

I watch him smile slowly in relief. He grabs the mic with both hands and starts to sway. In the corner of my eye I can see Talia getting impatient.

> *Broken glass*
> *It's nice to draw blood*
> *But don't drown in the abyss*
> *There is always a reason to get up again*
> *Rage chokes my throat*
> *Stabbed by a knife*
> *By the people who say they love you in the same breath*
> *It's bullshit.*

The song makes my hairs stand up on end. Goosebumps run up and down my arms. This awkward boy sang that? Did he write that? It's like a spark goes off in my head. I want them. I want them to play Riot Radio.

I'm pulled back to reality, with Talia, saying, "You're more indie, you should have auditioned with the indie bands."

I watch David's face fall. My chest tightens as I watch him begin to crumble. At that moment I wanted to to turn abruptly and hiss that she should shut the fuck up.

"I … I … talked to Sasha on air … and … I thought … we should audition here." he stammers.

"Well, you were wrong, you wasted our time." She says coldly.

I can't fucking take this. The look on David's face. His huge brown eyes are wide and his lips are quivering. I grab Talia by the shoulder and push her to the far side of the room to talk.

"The fuck is that about?" I snap.

"They auditioned in the wrong place," She hisses.

"Didn't you hear how good they were?" I hiss back.

"No and that's not my fault, I don't do indie." she says stiffly.

"Well, they were fucking great and I want them." I say my voice tight.

"Whatever you say, boss." she says mockingly. I walk away; I think I just made myself a fucking enemy.

We sit down again and Talia is pouting.

"Sorry about that you were great. You're in."

David's face lights up. "You really think so?" he asks eagerly. "No one has ever given us a chance."

"Fuck, yeah," I say, smiling.

"Sorry about auditioning in the wrong place," he says with wide, nervous eyes.

"Forget about it," I say warmly.

I'm watch him and his bandmates jump up and down with excitement when Cassandra leans in towards me.

"She doesn't know her fucking place," she whispers in my ear.

"I didn't think I was that kind of boss," I say simply.

"You're not, girl, she just has no respect."

She's right. I should have never fucked her. My hands clench tightly in annoyance at Talia and at myself.

"Hey hello. We are right fucking here," someone says.

We look up to see the lead singer of the next band waiting impatiently. He has long brown hair and wears a tight denim shirt and jeans. His hands are tattooed and he has silver rings on each finger.

My jaw tightens. "Go ahead." I resist the urge to jump over the table and punch that smirk right off his fucking face.

Their beat is faster than David's band. The guitars are meaner and louder. I should like this fucking band. I should love this fucking band. But its like I've heard them before. Like there's nothing special there. Like they are empty. The lyrics don't catch me. They sound … like … like they ripped off the fucking Black Keys. And their attitude is fucking pissing me off. I'm fucking done.

"Okay, stop." The way the singer looks at me sends chills down my spine. It's almost … predatory. I make myself as tall as possible, trying to pretend he doesn't faze me.

"What the fuck is the matter?" he demands. I sit straight up, my hands clenching into fists.

"I've heard it before." I say matter of factly.

"Well, what do the others think?" he snaps.

Cassandra leans her head on her tattooed hand. "Same here, hon."

"I didn't like it," Talia says.

"What the fuck is the matter with you bitches?" His hands slam on the table, his face way too close to mine. I force myself to be still. I can't show this asshole that I'm afraid. I won't let assholes like this take anything away from us. I won't.

I slam my hands down, too, and I get right in his face. I try to hide the fact that my hands are shaking. "Get the fuck out of my face asshole."

My eyes widen as his fist come close to my face. But before I can even react Taylor grabs him by the shoulders and punches him. I hear a scream rip from someone's throat. I feel myself double over with anxiety. Before the guy can lunge at us one of his bandmates holds him back and Steven is grabbing Taylor who is thrashing in his grip like a wild animal. I want to cry, but I force back my sobs and the fear that is running through me like tidal waves. I force my voice to be steady.

"Get out of my fucking radio station." I shout. His bandmates drag him away and everyone watches them, wide-eyed.

When they leave I straighten up, take a deep breath and say, "Let's keep fucking going." My jaw tightens and my hands shake badly. "Forget that asshole."

The next band is all girls, dressed in black leather and lace. Their lead singer is thick-limbed but carries herself like a fucking model. She has tanned skin, thick brown hair and she walks like she knows the band is going to blow us away.

"We are *The New Americana*, like the Halsey song," she says, her smouldering black, painted eyes taking us all in. She stands at the mic and the drummer calls out 'one-two-three-four!' The guitars come in searing and the beat is fast and vicious. She opens her mouth and a velvety smooth voice with an attitude belts out:

I tore my own heart in two
Its all my fucking fault
I want to wander down a path alone
With only the company of the moon.

The lyrics aren't what I expected from an all-girl punk band but somehow they make it work. I fucking want her … them … I want them.

"Stop," I say more to myself than the band. She glares at me and I try not to squirm. "I love it," I blurt out.

Cassandra gives me a knowing smile. I try to keep my face blank.

"I love your attitude," Cassandra says grinning, revealing her crooked and missing teeth.

"What did you think, Talia?" I ask, making a point of not looking at her.

"You guys were really good. We'll call you." I can't rip my gaze away from the singer and the way she moves, so gracefully.

"Sasha?" Cassandra says. I look over. "Next band, hon," she smiles.

We spend the day looking at bands sweat and stumble. Some get under my skin and I know I need to play them at my fucking radio station. It only takes a second for me to recognize something special about a band. I won't let anyone shake me—which is going to prove to be a dicey attribute, tomorrow, when we decide as a group which bands we want.

The day is finally over, and I'm in my apartment lying down with my eyes closed. *New Americana* is playing on repeat in my head. The lead singer's effortless movements, her smile and her attitude; her eyes that burn holes in my skin … and those lyrics.

I want to wander down a path alone, with
only the company of the moon.

It's gotten under my skin and in my brain. I picture her being close to me, our lips almost brushing. A cold feeling washes over me. I bolt upright, shaking hard.

No. No. No. I'm not doing this again. The kissing, the fucking, the drugs, the drinking. All the girls I've ever chosen are bad-asses. All the girls I've chosen fuck me up. They fuck me up and my dreams start fucking slipping away. Never again.

I curl up in a tight ball and try to block out the world for a few hours. I wake up suddenly to a knock at the door. I make my way over the records and books to get to the door. I fling it open and see Ben and Taylor.

"Uh … hey," I say.

"Um," Taylor said. "I … I just wanted to apologize for yesterday." he mumbles.

"It's okay, you did what I wanted to do," I say.

"I have a chocolate banana apology muffin." I take the bag enjoying the smell. "From the Purple Penguin, your favourite," Taylor says, smiling nervously at me.

"You're forgiven. Come in." I say.

Taylor smiles in relief and I can see his whole body relax.

I rush to put on clothes and grab my bag. When we get to Riot Radio, I see everyone else is waiting.

"Sorry we are late." I pant.

"You're the boss, hon—that means we're early," Cassandra says, giving me one her reassuring smiles.

"Okay, let's talk bands," I say, "Cassandra, tell the boys what we decided." I watch Taylor's eyes brighten at casually being referred to as a boy.

I made sure that Cassandra, Talia and I did the selection process together. I want them to feel they have a say in what we do here. First, we made sure their music style fits what we are looking for. If not, they can fucking forget it.

We analyzed their style and their talent. Also, they had to be able to fucking sing. And they can't be assholes. I'm not working with assholes. Or homophobes. Definitely not!

We chose the Riot Grrrl band because they were badass and worship the same musicians we do. Plus, they had some real fucking talent. *New Americana* got in my fucking head and we could all agree they had something special. Queer core had fucking everything. I want them all to play on my station.

"We chose … drum roll …" Steven does a drum roll on the desk, "The Riot Grrrl group, Queer Core and The New Americana! Please, hold your applause," Cassandra says, smiling with her with her arms sweeping wide. We all laugh. But my laugh is fucking fake.

"Guys what did you decide for the indie bands?" I listen to them rattle off the indie bands they liked.

"Okay, good," I say. "Ben, you call the indie bands and Cassandra you call the punk bands." Then I motion to Talia. "Talia, we're going on the air."

I lean in and we go on the air. I say, "We had a lot of people come play yesterday. Thanks everyone for coming. If you are pissed you didn't get called back, get over yourself or try again next time. Listen in next week … Friday we are going to start playing the bands."

The comment board lights up.

"You're on the air." I say.

"Remember me?" Chills race down my spine. I recognize the voice. It's the asshole from the auditions. "You didn't give us a fucking chance. I'm coming for you when you don't have your fucking bodyguards."

I freeze, anxiety rallying against my flesh, everything becomes fuzzy around the edges. I grip the table to stop from passing out. I hear Talia's voice on the air.

"You go near her and we will rip you in two," she shoots back.

I sway hard and I lose my grip. I feel myself falling and pain explodes in my head. Everything goes black.

I open my eyes to everything aching. I'm wrapped in a thick blanket on my coveted black velvet couch.

"Here hon, drink this. It's vanilla tea with wild honey." Cassandra says as she hands me the cup.

"Thank you," I mumble, my head pounding.

"We called the police on his ass," Taylor says. "They are watching out for him."

I manage to nod.

"We'll take care of everything today," Talia says.

"Rest up. You will have endless cups of tea and good music," Cassandra says.

"Thanks." I drink the tea letting it warm my insides. I bury myself in the blanket, blocking myself from the world.

"Hey, time to go." I open my eyes to Ben lifting me up. "Let's go home," he says. I nod and I let him help me. "Cassandra says you can borrow the blanket."

"Okay." I say weakly.

Walking down the street, Ben puts my arm over his shoulder. I don't deserve him. I don't deserve any of them.

CHAPTER 20

I THINK THIS IS ROCK BOTTOM ... IT'S KINDA LONELY DOWN HERE

wake up thinking it's morning. It's only 12:30 a.m. I get up and find I'm shaking, hard. I still see that asshole from the audition. I can't get that sneering face out of my head. The predatory look, his voice taunting me. I stumble to the toilet and my stomach heaves. My throat burns as I lean back on the cold tiles. I reach desperately into my pocket. The drugs I got from that sleaze bag drug dealer, Darren, are still there. I rip it open and put it on my tongue. For one moment, for one fucking moment, I think of spitting it out. I close my mouth, letting it dissolve on my tongue. I let it take me away from my shaking limbs. I let it take me away from here.

I wake up to a knock at my door. I must have fallen asleep on the bathroom floor and now its cold pierces my skin. My bones ache and my brain pulses behind my skull. I manage to stand up and stagger to the door. It's Ben, with that smile and a coffee. For a minute I want to snap at him that I don't need him to wake me up and to get the fuck out of my apartment. I swallow it down.

"Hey, Ben."

"I just wanted to check in on you after yesterday," he says with his warm smile. Usually, that smile makes everything better. But not today, not today.

"I'm fine," I mutter.

"You look like shit," he says.

"I couldn't sleep," I answer.

"You okay to come in today?" I want to say 'no'. I want to stay home. I want to get fucked up.

"I'm going to try," I say instead.

"You need any help?" he asks.

"No, I'm good. I'll meet you there."

I never made it there. I throw myself onto my bed. I can feel it all slipping away. Everything that holds me together is slipping away and I can't reach it. I can't hold onto it. I just can't. I know what I can do. I get up. I fumble with my black Converse sneakers and go out into the biting cold. It jars through my bones, but I can't bring myself to care.

I see him. His head is bald, with a tattoo of a snake coming from his forehead down past his neck. He is wearing dirty red jeans and a dirty leather vest. He wreaks of rot, decay, rock bottom.

"Darren." I call. He looks up at me like I'm something to taste. It makes me nauseous. It makes me want to run.

"Haven't seen you in a while." His tongue licks his yellow rotting teeth.

"I'm here now," I say. Hating every fucking word.

"What do you want?" he asks, tilting his head, his snake-like tongue darting in and out.

"Anything that can make me forget." I say.

"I forgot how interesting our visits were."

My stomach churns in disgust. At him and at me. "Just give me the drugs. I got the money."

He hands it to me and I snatch it from him.

"If you do something for me, I'll give you extra," he says, breathing stench in my ear and making all my hairs stand on end.

"Fuck you!" I say stumbling away. Darren laughs, showing his missing teeth. "You were always feisty."

"Fuck off."

I go to the liquor store and stare at the bottles. The fluorescent lights dig into my skull. Rock bottom, fluorescent lights are rock bottom. I'm trying to remember which booze makes me forget everything. Vodka. It's vodka. That I remember.

I grab a bottle and go to the cash. The clerk squints at me with beady black eyes. I'm too out of it to care. "ID?" I nod fumbling around for my fake ID. I push it over, trying to keep myself steady. He takes his time examining the small piece of plastic. "Okay. Fifteen bucks," he finally says. I give him the crumpled bills and I stagger out.

When I get home, I greedily open the bottle of vodka and chug it down, letting the liquid warm my insides, letting it blur everything. I drink until I can't see. Until I can't think. I curl up with the bottle by my side. I let the blackness take me under. Who was I to think I deserve anything?

The door flings open, ramming into the wall. Dark figures run in. I can barely open my eyes.

"Sasha, its me - Ben. Get up."

"Ben?" I croak out.

"Get up."

"No. No. No." Desperation fills my breakable frame until I'm shaking. I don't want to get up. Why won't they let me waste away? Don't they fucking see I don't want to be here anymore? I don't want to be here. I feel hands lift me up. I want to break free, but I can't seem to get my limbs to move.

"I'll help her get some clothes on."

"Cassandra?" I murmur. "What the fuck is happening?"

"Let's get some clothes on you, honey," she says, her voice full of concern. I can feel her stripping my tank top off my greasy, sweaty skin and putting sweatpants and a clean shirt on me.

"You got a jacket, hon?" she says softly.

"Yeah," I whisper. "Closet." I watch her go through the clothes in my closet. She grabs the leather jacket with the hoodie inside, the only warm jacket I have. She puts it on me and wraps her arms around my body, supporting me. I feel safe for the first time in weeks. Then she gently takes me outside my apartment.

"What's going on? What's going on?" I ask, rocking back and forth. "Shhh, hon, it's okay." I let them take me down the stairs and outside into the biting cold.

I can feel it now. I know the route, we are going to Riot Radio. Fear spikes, in every single nerve. I don't want to go back there.

"No. No. No!" I scream, cold air tearing through my lungs. "Don't take me back there!"

Fat tears roll down my cheeks. I'm shaking harder now. I try to break free. I thrash in Cassandra's arms, but she is much stronger than I am. I'm screaming for her to let me go. Just let me go. I scratch at her arms. Ben grabs my hands, firmly but gently at the same time. Tears stream down my face as they get me through the door of Riot Radio. I see everyone sitting in a circle. A fucking intervention.

A fucking intervention!

Cassandra sits me down carefully.

"Sasha, we're worried about you," Ben says.

I can't respond. I'm shaking too hard and the sobs are keeping me from being able to speak.

"Tell us what's going on," he says, pleading.

I'm sobbing harder now. I still can't speak. Finally, I find my voice. "I've been getting fucked up." My words catch and break. It's all I can manage.

"What does that mean?" Ben asks, still pleading.

I want to run, run and disappear. Disappear, where no one can find me and I can finish this destruction for good this time.

"Drinking a lot … and … and …"

Cassandra's heavily tattooed hand holds mine tight. "Go ahead, hon."

"Getting high. Not eating. Trying to die."

"Has this happened before?" Ben whispers, tears forming in those beautiful blue eyes.

"Yes." I say softly.

"Fuck, how could I have not seen this?" he murmurs.

Ben paces, muttering under his breath. "How could I have not seen this? How could I have not seen this?" he repeats. He stops. "*Why* did this happen?" he asks, his voice cracking. "Why did this happen, Sasha?" his voice breaks this time.

"I slipped. I slipped. I slipped." I can't stop saying it, like I'm a broken record. I start rocking back and forth violently. Tears fall, too fast.

"We have to take her," Cassandra says.

"Yeah. We do." Ben whispers, his hands rubbing his face.

Take me? They want to lock me up like I'm crazy. I'm not crazy. I'm just broken. A broken girl that needs to be put together again.

"No!" I shout, slicing the quiet tension. Everyone turns to look at me, surprise and sympathy in their eyes. That fucking sympathy.

"I can … I can …" I force my voice to steady. "I can do it myself. I've done it before."

Cassandra comes over and takes my hands. "You need help, hon." There are tears in her eyes. I don't want to see tears, especially tears over me.

"Help me then," I whimper. "Don't take Riot Radio from me," I cry, choking on my words. "It is the only thing I care about it." I can't stand the sound of my desperation. I bury my head in my hands. "You guys and Riot Radio are all that matter. I don't want to lose it. I don't want to lose all of you," I plead, my face still in my hands.

I've never been like this, desperate, pleading. I would rather fucking die.

I watch Ben take a deep breath. "Let's give her a month," he suggests looking anxiously at the others.

All the tension leaves my shoulders and I slump over in relief. They're not taking me away. They're not taking me away. There's still hope for Riot Radio.I'm rocking back and forth. This raw fear, eating away everything. I can feel my broken pieces pressing against my rib cage like glass. I can't fuck this up. I can't fuck up anymore.

I feel arms around me holding me close. I open my eyes to Ben. Ben, crying into my shoulder. His tears staining my leather jacket. He's shaking. Its like he loves me. "I'm not going to lose you," he whispers in my ear.

I want to say, 'you won't, but I don't want to be a liar.

I open my eyes wide to the sound of my alarm. It pierces my brain, making my head ache. On first instinct, I reach under my bed for a bottle. Then I remember I'm not fucking up anymore.

Panic jars my bones. What will I do when I'm drowning in the thick sadness or when the fear is eating away at me? I bite my tongue to stop the scream from escaping my mouth. There's a rusty taste of blood in my mouth. I'm about to go off the edge when there's a soft knock on the door. I force my voice to come out of my mouth and say, "Come in." Ben comes in and I grab the sheets tight to keep from crying. Every time I would break, no one bothered to pick up the pieces but me and now I have people who care that I get put back together the right way. It's almost more than I can bear.

"I brought you your favourite: grilled cheese, chocolate banana muffin and a latte." Ben smiles, but it's not the same. The light in his smile is weaker—and I did that to him. It makes my stomach turn and my grip tightens so I don't have to feel all this.

"Um … do you want to come into work today?" He can't even look at me. Like he broke me, like I am all his fault.

"Yeah, I do," I whisper. "Ben, look at me." I plead. I just want to see the warmth in his blue eyes. It will make everything better. I force myself not to cry out when it's not there.

"Ben, this is not your fault," I whisper. Regret colours everything. My words, my face; it eclipses everything I'm feeling.

"I should have seen it. I should have seen it, Sasha. I fucking gave you drinks and I ... I never fucking asked if the threats on Riot Radio affected you. They fucking affected me! At one point I didn't want to be gay anymore. I didn't bother to come talk to you and you are right next door! I was fucking next door and I didn't do shit. I'm a fucking asshole!" I can feel salty tears run into my mouth as I watch Ben cry. My hands tighten around his to make him look at me.

"Ben, without you, I probably ... I probably ... sobs catch in my throat ... would have killed myself," I whisper the last part. It's too much to say it out loud.

I watch the tears fall down Ben's face and his shoulders shake in silent sobs. I hate that he's crying ... crying because of me. I take him in my arms and he rests his head on my lap and I fucking hold him tight as he sobs. He is too precious to break.

We walk into Riot Radio hand in hand. Everyone turns their heads, taking us in. "Are you guys ... like an item now?" Timothy asks. His eyes narrow and his nose scrunches up.

We both laugh and it feels so fucking good not to cry.

"No, we are still both as gay as rainbows. Ben and I are family," I say. "We are all family." I climb up on the desk, spreading my arms wide. And we are going to be the biggest underground operation this world has ever fucking seen!" I yell.

Everyone cheers and at that moment I know things will get better. Fuck that's fucking cheesy. Ha. Not sorry.

Talia comes toward us, her black-painted greenish-blue eyes in slits. "Back so soon?" she asks.

Dread makes my stomach churn. I thought it was me falling apart that caused this feeling. I still feel it when I look at her, like the worst is yet to come. I can make a choice, just wait it out and keep my eye on her or I can be a bad bitch now. I'm tired of breaking and feeling people step on the pieces like I'm fucking nothing.

"Ya,I'm back, Talia. Move over, that's my fucking spot," I say, my head held high. I can see Cassandra wink at me from the corner of my eye.

I tense when I see the mess on the control station. Usually, I have empty coffee cups and food wrappers around, but this is fucking worse. Goth and metal albums litter the control station.

"Talia. What the fuck is this?" I demand, my anger boiling up inside of me, wanting a way out. I wave a record in her face. "Have you been playing this shit?"

To her credit, she doesn't flinch. Her eyes narrow and she gets in my space. "Yeah, so fucking what?" she demands. "I kept this place alive while you were gone."

"I fucking told you what kind of music we play," I say, my voice and body tensing up.

"We have not had one single threat from our new listeners. They aren't cave people like you punks." she sneers.

Punk saved my fucking life. It *is* my fucking life. How dare that little bitch say that about punks?

"You took advantage because you are the only one who knows how to work the control station," I spit.

"It's not my fault you are a fucking drug-addicted alcoholic!" she throws back.

Something in me just snapped. I slap her hard. She pulls back, holding her cheek. Before I can move, her fist collides with my nose. Blood gushes down my face and into my mouth. I punch her back through the blood. Her nails dig into my skin, she pushes me and my back hits the cement ground. There's no time to cry out; her nails are going for my face.

Taylor grabs hold of her and pulls her away from me. I watch her head go back and collide with Taylor's jaw. He cries out and she breaks free, staring down at me. She is breathing hard and looking at me like she fucking won. I won't let it end like this, with that bitch staring down at me. I wince as I get up, pain is shooting through my back.

"You are fucking fired!" I scream.

"Good. This station is shit," she says getting in my face. "I will fucking destroy you, Sasha."

"Get the fuck out of my face!" I shout.

Cassandra comes and stands in front of me. "You heard her, get out," she says.

I flip her off with a black-painted nail.

"I'm going to destroy you all. Boom!" she says, giving us a wicked grin.

I watch her walk away. I thought the dread would be finally gone, but it's still growing.

"Hello, freaks and more freaks. I know you haven't heard my voice in a while. I fucking apologize for all the goth music. The bitch who played it is dead. Don't worry, not literally, but there were some blows exchanged. I've been dealing with a lot of shit lately. Listen, if you're going through shit, turn up the fucking music and tell someone. No fucking shame in it. I wouldn't be here if it wasn't for my family here at Riot Radio. Fucking shout-out to all who work here and making Riot Radio what it is. I fucking love you all. Here's a song about fucking falling apart, *Blame,* by Bully."

For a moment I just sit there listening to Bully on my giant retro headphones. I just want to stay in that moment, listening to a kick-ass song I picked and having hundreds of listeners listen to it along with me. But I know peace like this doesn't last.

The board lights up. "You're on Riot Radio."

"Hey, it's Tanya, from *New Americana.* Can't wait to play on your station. When can we play?"

"You could have just called me directly."

"And not use this airtime to get publicity for my band? No way." I laugh.

"You'll hear *New Americana* soon on Riot Radio and a lot of other kick-ass bands, too."

"Looking forward to it, Riot Radio," she says.

I can feel a smile tugging at my lips. From the corner of my eye, I can see Cassandra giving me a knowing look.

"Hey, Sasha." I look up to see Ben's concerned blue eyes taking up my world. I can get lost in eyes that actually give a fuck about me. "Hey, just checking in on what went down with Talia. Please be honest."

Ben's pleading with me. No one's ever wanted my honesty, just my carefully constructed lies.

"I've always had a bad feeling about her," I whispered. "What hurts is that I fucked her when I knew … when I fucking knew it wasn't right. I'm just fucked up. I always will be." I try to hold down the tears.

Ben's hands tighten on mine. "I don't see that. I see a strong, badass girl who is passionate about what she does. Who would do anything for the people she cares about. That's what I see."

"Ben you're gonna make me cry. Shit! I am crying." And, I'm fucking smiling all at the same time.

CHAPTER 21

I'M BACK FROM ROCK BOTTOM AND I SLAPPED A BITCH

I'M looking in the mirror. All I see is a girl with grey skin and bones jutting out of her face. I'm fucking trying to see the girl Ben talked about. This strong girl. I don't see her at all.

I wake up in the morning and I'm back to the mirror. I put on foundation and blush with a shaky hand. I don't want to see this dying girl anymore. I put red lipstick on. I want to see the leader of fucking Riot Radio in this mirror. She's in there somewhere. I'm going to fucking find her.

For the first time in a long time, I knock on Ben's door. It takes him a few minutes to answer. Ben's curly, raven hair is a mess and it looks like he just threw on his clothes.

"Hey ... Sasha," he says looking surprised to see me.

"One-night stand last night, huh Ben?" I ask, faking a laugh. Because that's what the old Sasha would do, laugh at that shit cause she thinks it's funny. Now I just want to make sure no one breaks his fucking heart. Ben's too good for this world, for a one-night stand shit. I freeze when I see Taylor wearing a black binder and not much else. Both their faces are pale. It's happening again. My friends will be wrapped up in each other and forget how much I need them.

I fake a smile. The old Sasha would make a joke of it, sweep it aside. Do I want her back? Deep down she was broken, just waiting to fall apart. The new Sasha is raw from the stitches that were used to put her back together.

"You're ... you're not going to fire us, are you?" Taylor asks, looking right through my fake smile.

"No ... of course not. Just don't fuck on my couch and it's all good."

They can see right fucking through it ... but neither of them says a fucking word.

"To work, boys."

I'm fiddling with the controls at work thinking of Ben and Taylor. I need them both to help me keep the pieces together. I need to throw myself into Riot Radio and focus on how much this station needs me.

The board is starting to light up.

"Hello, you fucking weirdos, how's it going? I'm gonna play some punk love shit today because us weirdos fall in love and lust too y'know?"

I look up at Ben and Taylor giving me shy smiles. I grin and wink just like the old Sasha would do and for that moment I was her again.

The board is lighting up like crazy.

"You're on Riot Radio."

"Hey, I've been listening to Riot Radio for a long time and you guys don't play goth stuff anymore." "There's a new station that plays it. What the fuck Riot Radio?"

"This has and will always be a punk and indie station," I say, my voice tight.

Cassandra is suddenly beside me and whispers, "What station?"

"What fucking station?" I ask.

"They're right across from you guys on Queen Street, I'll be listening to them from now on."

The fuck? We all scramble to the window and there it is. Black Hole Radio. In front of the building having a smoke is … Talia.

My stomach heaves as I see Jamie and Sophia come out of the building. Jamie with a smoke in hand and a sneer on his face and Sophia saying something to Talia.

It's not enough that they insult me and try to break me. They have to work for the fucking enemy. This is war.

Wait, how did she get a radio station? This is fucking Queen St East! That fucking bitch must be loaded.

"That fucking bitch," Cassandra snarls. "Do you want me to go over there and fuck her up?" asks Cassandra still snarling.

"Fucking tempting," I mutter. Then, "Fucking team meeting," I announce. Everyone gathers, looking at me with wide, anxious eyes.

"I know this fucking sucks, but no one is to go over there. We will kick her ass from in here."

"Maybe we should branch out a little," Taylor suggests.

I fight down the anger and bitterness that want their way out.

"I'm not fucking losing our integrity over her."

"But … we could play more indie," he suggests.

"Ok Taylor, you are in charge of finding new indie stuff to play." He nods like I've imparted a great duty on him. I kind of have.

"I know who can help with that." We all turn to look at Timothy who rarely says anything. "I've been texting David, the singer from the indie band we chose." He says with a smile big enough to split his face. "He can come to help us out." He looks down at his phone … "now actually."

"Good work."

"What's Riot Radio going to be?" I yell.

"The biggest fucking underground operation in the world!" Everyone yells back.

"Fucking right! Let's get to work!" I say.

I go over to the control station and fiddle with the controls, thinking about what to say.

"Hello, freaks. I'm going to go kinda soft right now and say, if you are ever fucking suffering for any reason tell someone. Your partner, your best friend, your family, your fucking cat. Just let it out and if you are still fucking struggling, get help. Put your fucking favourite song on and push through. I'm going to play *Creature Comfort* by Arcade Fire, a song about mental health and the fucked-up expectations society places on us. If you don't fucking like it, I don't fucking care."

Then I added, "I just said fuck a lot. I just realized that. Ha. I don't a give a fuck."

"*Arcade Fire*. Cool." I look up to see David sitting on a desk next to me swinging his legs, wearing tight red jeans.

"Timothy texted saying you guys need help on the indie front," he says with a lopsided grin. "I always loved you guys, but I always wished you played more indie. Sorry ... I don't mean to tell you guys what to do," he says, looking down and blushing slightly.

"Fuck, no. I wanna to hear what people have to say."

"Since when? You always say you don't give a fuck what people think. I mean it's cool and all ... but yeah, accepting feedback is a good thing."

"I agree ... plus we got fucking competition."

"Competition? What? Who?" David asks, his eyes wide.

"Look behind you," I say. I watch him take in Black Hole Radio. "Talia opened her own station."

David jumps down from the desk, raises one hand in the air, places one on his guitar and says, "I pledge allegiance to this radio station. I swear on my guitar that I will do everything in my power to help you crush Black Hole."

"Thank you, brave, young knight, for helping us slay the fucking bitch."

"You're welcome, my queen," he says, winking.

"Taylor!" I call. He comes over, assessing David. "David will help you with the indie side of things."

"Does he work here now?" Taylor asks with a little suspicion in his voice.

I understand. When you have a family, you don't want anyone screwing up a good thing.

"I don't want a job but … um … I *would* like a favour," he explains.

"Name it," I say. I watch Taylor's eyes burn as if he's guarding me against the evil of David asking for a favour.

"I want our band to play first," he says.

"Deal," I say.

"Cool," he replies with that lopsided grin.

"This is for you."

I look up to see Timothy pushing an album into my hands. I see the name *Taco Cat* on the cover.

"They love cats and tacos," Timothy says matter-of-factly.

"Yeah, I can see that."

"It's a good place to start," he says solemnly. This isn't the first time someone imparted music wisdom on me, but it gets me every time. I fight hard not to cry.

"They're a bit punky and offbeat—like you," he says, tilting his head and smiling.

"Um … thanks. I think."

"It's a compliment," Timothy says, "One freak to another." He grins and takes my hands.

"Thanks," I say, smiling for real, for the first time in a long time. One freak to another.

The next day I'm clutching the *Taco Cat* record. The cover is full of different-coloured cat clocks. Punks would laugh at this shit. I would have laughed at this shit. I sigh. Indie kids need this as much as the punk rock kids. A place that gets you. A place where you can disappear and feel fucking better about whatever shit is going on in your life.

I take out the record, place it on the turntable and lay down the needle. I listen to the opening guitar licks. The first song has a punk beat and is about the lead woman from the X-Files. The second is a 'fuck you' to periods.

It's so fucking weird and punky. I'm fucking sold.

I'm taking a sip of my latte and looking at the back cover when Ben walks in. "I've got bagels boss lady," he announces.

"They better be covered in cream cheese or I'm cutting your head off and am going to display it on my control centre," I tease.

Ben sits on the desk next to me dangling his legs and grinning like David did yesterday. "That's fucking dark," he says, but he's laughing.

"Gotta balance out after this record cover," I say pushing *Taco Cat* towards him.

"Fucking weird cover. Was it any good?" he asks, tilting his head slightly.

"It was surprisingly good," I say.

"Let's put it on before everyone gets here," Ben says. He leans over me and puts the record on the turntable. He's close, closer than he's ever been. His eyes are fucking beautiful. I have never seen eyes that look like midnight. I can smell his signature scent of almonds and vanilla. His lips are a pale pink. He's perfect. Unexpectedly his hand tightens over mine. His lips pressing against mine. I find myself kissing him back. The door opens and we pull back like we've been burned.

"Hey, guys," Taylor says, oblivious to what just happened. "How's *Taco Cat*?" he asks.

"Um … uh … really good. I'm gonna play it today," I say, trying to steady my voice.

"Cool."

Ben glances at me. We share the same look. What the fuck have we done? He's with Taylor—and me … I don't know about me. I lean back in my chair while everyone gets ready for the day. I'm gay as fuck. Ben is gay as fuck. But … it felt kind of right at that moment. I never wanted to kiss Jamie.

My hands start to shake itching for the cold of a bottle or something melting on my tongue. I place my hands on the control board, hoping the familiar feel will stop the shaking. It's eight-thirty, time to go on the air.

"Hey die-hard fans and insomniacs, we're fucking doing something different! We are playing some indie punk. All you indie kids out there, you are not fucking alone! We punk rock freaks are here for you. Now, for the first time on Riot Radio, here is *Taco Cat*."

"Ben," I hiss. He turns his head and there are those eyes that make my chest ache. "We need to talk." He nods and we go outside. I feel tears hot in my eyes.

"We can't do this," I whisper through my tears.

"You felt something too," he whispers.

"Yes." I let out a long breath.

"We can't do this … you have Taylor," I say. "He's too good to be broken."

"I know," he nods, tears in his eyes too.

"I have to focus on my mental health and Riot Radio," I say, trying to steady my voice.

"I know," he whispers.

He takes my hands. "I will always love you, as my friend."

"You are not going to leave me, are you?" I say softly. "I need you."

"I'm going to be by your side forever," he says. "Okay?"

"Okay."

"Let's go inside."

I nod. Once inside I see my board has lit up with calls.

"You're on the air." I'm getting comments like:

"I fucking loved *Taco Cat*."

"Indie has so many good girl bands."

"It's fucking awesome that you're playing more indie."

"Do you have any bands you want us to play?" I ask, trying to steady myself. Still reeling from what happened with Ben. "Riot

Radio is taking requests. I can't fucking believe it. This station is going to be a home for all fucked-up kids," I say. "That's always what I wanted it to be."

"You should play K. Flay. She's fucking awesome."

I write 'K.Flay' on a notepad.

"Consider it done. You're on the air."

"I heard you guys have some competition. Black hole. What the fuck is that all about?"

"A disgruntled ex-employee decided to make her own station," I sneer. "Alt goth stuff," I spit out.

"You're not going to play that shit to compete, are you?" the voice asks warily.

"Fuck, no. Riot Radio will be an enteral home for all fucked-up punk and indie kids. We won't fucking abandon you," I say my voice steady now.

"Good, this fucking station is the only thing that keeps me together." You and me both I think to myself. "We aren't fucking going anywhere."

"Good. Stay fucking weird."

"You too … You are on the air."

"What the fuck were you playing?"

"That was *Taco Cat*," I say my body tensing, ready to fight.

"That wasn't punk. They are fucking posers."

"I don't know if you fucking heard me, this is an indie station as well as punk."

"I know a bunch of faggots work for you, but you don't have to play their music."

I freeze up, my stomach heaves. I don't want to be that girl anymore, the one that threatens her listeners. I want to be their fucking saviour—or at least the reason they are still here.

I can't speak. I can't speak. I smell lavender and feel Cassandra's warmth around me. She leans into the mic and says, "We are pro LGBTQ plus here. If you don't like that, get the fuck away from our station. Sincerely, a faggot."

I bolt outside. I need some fresh air. I breathe the cold air into my lungs. I need to be able to say what Cassandra said, it was perfect. I need be able to deal with assholes without falling apart.

I stiffen as I see Talia walk out of her building and get a cigarette from her purse. I can't let her see me weak … vulnerable. I cross my arms and work my face into a sneer. She flips one perfectly black manicured nail at me. I flip one of my broken nails with chipping black paint at her. Neither of us wants to back down.

I can't believe I let her get to me to the point where I was breaking again. She's not fucking worth it.

The cold air raises the hairs on my arms as I look at her cold stare. I shake my head. I'm done with this. My fucking radio station will speak for itself.

That night I'm in my bed, covers up tight to my face, googling K.Flay. I'm hooked after the first song. *Blood in the Cut*. A song about your crush fucking someone else.

Her style isn't anything I've heard before. Rap mixed with Indie.

She sings about addiction, needing to forget, your love being with someone else. The fear of not being fucking good enough. It's like she was *made* for the listeners of Riot Radio.

The next morning, I play the insistent thunder of *Blood in a Cut as* I look in my mirror trying to look as dangerous as this song. Not like K.Flay—she insists in her lyrics that she follows the rules, that she isn't bad. That's not me. That will never be me. That's not who us punk rock freaks are. We want to destroy things, burn them down and build them up from the ashes.

I cover my eyes with thick black eyeliner, inspired by Sid Vicious' girlfriend, Nancy. My torn white tank reads, 'Fuck You' and my tight black jeans are full of holes and sliver safety pins.

I put on my black leather jacket and stick my headphones in. I'm playing *High Enough* by K.Flay.

> *I'm already high enough*
> *I only have eyes for you*

These lyrics are playing when I see him. I keep my head down trying to walk faster, but he catches up to me. I let out a breath through my clenched teeth. I can feel the stench of his breath on my neck. My drug dealer … former drug dealer.

"Hello, little Sasha. Where have you been? Trying to better yourself?"

His voice sends ice-cold shivers down my spine.

"I'll scream," I whisper. I'm holding back tears. My hands are starting to shake. He clamps his hand on my mouth. It tastes like dirt, sweat and desperation. I can feel the tears soaking my cheeks now. What would I tell the listeners of Riot Radio to do? What would that Sasha do?

Kick his ass.

I bite down hard on his hand and taste blood as my teeth dig into his skin. He lets out a scream and I stomp my black Doc Marten boot down on his foot. I whirl around, out of his grip, and punch him in the jaw. He falls down. I look at his skin-and-bones body and kick him in the stomach until he screams.

People start crowding around us and I break out into a run as fast as my black boots will take me.

I'm the first one at Riot Radio and my heart races too fast in my chest as I lock myself inside. My vision blurs and everything gets dark. I clutch my control center hard to stay on my feet. I want to forget. I need to forget. My hands search under the panel of buttons for the familiar bottle. It's still there! I'm about to open it up when I feel arms around me. The smell of vanilla and almonds, the feel of soft curly hair against my face. Ben.

"Ben." My voice breaks and the tears come, soaking his blue, plaid top.

"Don't talk, just let me hold you," he whispers.

He holds my shaking body until I go still and limp in his arms.

A few hours later with some of my sanity gathered, I'm on the air.

"I just discovered the female badass, K.Flay. She's a blend of rap and indie. If you don't like it, get the fuck off my station."

"The message board lights up right away.

"You're on Riot Radio."

"What if I do have a problem with it? Are you going to beat me like that guy on Queen Street West? Bash my face in?" It's a girl's voice. And it's familiar. Too familiar. My voice is tight and I'm shaking hard.

"You know who this is. Shut down this station or I'm calling the cops."

The line goes dead. My breathing starts going faster and faster until I can't see. The room starts to spin and tears fall. I feel strong arms holding me for the second time today.

"She's not going to touch you." It's Cassandra's velvety rich voice reassuring me.

"She's not really going to call the cops, is she?" Taylor's asks.

"No, because we're going to fuck her up first," Cassandra declares.

"Cassandra, she's not worth it," Ben's warns.

"Cassandra is not going to jail for defending herself against that scum," I say. Through my blurred vision, I see Cassandra grab one of the gas cans that Steven stores here for his motorcycle.

"Fuck, no. Cassandra, don't!" I plead.

Ben moves toward her and Taylor grabs his shoulder.

"Let her go," he murmurs.

I struggle to get up and my knees give away. The world spins and I cry out. I see Cassandra taking long, determined strides in her tight, black, leather pants, her long white-blonde hair swinging back and forth. The lights from Riot Radio illuminate her tall figure under the onyx night sky. She is heading toward Black Hole Radio. Her sliver boots glinting in the night.

We all stand frozen in the doorway of Riot Radio. For a moment I see nothing—then I see Cassandra throw her sliver lighter towards the Black Hole.

My ears hear the explosion first, then flames erupt into the night sky. I cover my ears with my hands. The flames grow, consuming everything in their path, taking Black Hole Radio with them.

Cassandra stumbles back, her eyes wide, the flames roaring behind her, finishing the destruction she began.

"We never speak of this again," Taylor whispers in the darkness.

"Everybody get the fuck out of here!" I scream. "No one is getting arrested tonight."

Alone in the station, the image of Cassandra's figure walking into the night towards Black Hole Radio with a can of gas, replays over and over in my head. I should have done more to try and stop it. Tell them it's a fucking stupid and crazy idea. Tell them it's wrong… tell them …

I groan as I cover my face with my hands, *Fuck!* " Talia will suspect me. We are fucking rivals, after all. I'd cover for Cassandra in a heartbeat. At least that's what I want to believe. They are my fucking family … I can't let anything happen to them. I can't.

"Fuck, what am I going to do? What am I going to do?" I mutter as I pace back and forth.

It hit me so hard it shook my body. I fucking know what to do.

This is the only way to save us. Even if I have to give up everything to do it. A stray tear rolls down my cheek. I created this all on my own and now I'm going to destroy it.

I take in everything, my control station, my crates of records, the old desks everyone works at, my prized black velvet couch and all the leather that Timothy used to make this place look more kickass.

It's time to burn it to the ground.

I take the other red container of gas and pour it over everything. My eyes narrow, my jaw juts out, determined. My chest heaves. I'm shaking with rage that it had to come to this. I walk out, not looking back. A flame jumps out of my black and silver lighter as I throw it behind me.

Fuck you, Talia!

I watch flames reach into the night for the second time. I thought I'd be fucking torn up. I thought I'd be sad or furious. I feel nothing. Fucking nothing!

CHAPTER 22

WHEN YOUR HOPES AND DREAMS ARE LITERALLY BURNED TO THE GROUND

I made sure the next day that I was the last one to show up at Riot Radio. Or what's left of it. This time a tear does fall. What the fuck have I done? I see everyone standing behind the yellow caution tape. Ben has tears filling his fucking beautiful eyes. He has his hand tight around Taylor's. Timothy and Steven are talking in whispers. I can feel Cassandra's eyes boring into me. I manage to look up. That look … she knows.

I'm about to go into a full panic attack when she nods … as if saying it was the only thing we could have done. Like she would have done the same if she was me.

My blood freezes when I see Talia coming towards us. How can I ever forget that lavender hair and those greenish-blue painted eyes? She is walking fast in knee-high leather boots. The urge to murder me is all over her face. Cassandra and Taylor step in front of me, trying to guard me from whatever Talia is planning to do.

"You fucking bitch!" she snarls. "You got one of your little faggots to burn down my fucking radio station!" she screams, disgust colouring her whole face.

I take a deep breath, I have to be fucking convincing, every word counts. The tears are falling fast now. I'm starting to mourn what I did to the best thing I have ever done.

"Do you …" I choke back a sob, "Do you fucking think I would do this to my own fucking radio station? You did this!" I scream back.

I watch Talia take in what's left of Riot Radio for the first time.

"Fuck," she murmurs. She shakes her head, hard.

"You're fucking crazy! You did this!" she screams, her face red, her eyes widening, her chest heaving.

"I built this place from the ground up on my fucking own!" I yell. "I want to kill whoever did this!" I say, my whole body shaking hard.

"You are a fucking liar!" she screams.

Before I can react, I feel her sharp nails graze my cheek, drawing blood. Then I swing at her. She avoids my fist and then lunges at me. Cassandra wraps her arms tight around her. Talia fights hard, trying to crush Cassandra's feet, dig her nails into her skin.

"She isn't calming down, someone call 911." Cassandra's voice is hoarse, but calm like there isn't an insane goth girl thrashing in her arms.

Within minutes, the police arrive. I take in the scene. Blood is pounding in my ears. I can't hear a fucking thing. The sight of the red and blue lights pulse in my skull. Cassandra finally lets go, Talia keeps screaming. Because she's acting so out of control, a policeman grabs her. She frantically tries to escape the arms of the policeman while giving me a murderous glare.

Then sound comes rushing back full force.

"She burned down my fucking radio station!" Talia screams.

I sink to the ground … this is it.

"Officer, as you can see, we came here to find our station burned down, as well," Cassandra says calmly.

The officers nod, question all of us and ease a now-limp Talia into a police car. We all watch the car drive away.

"It's over," I whisper. "It's all over."

"What about the station?" Ben asks full of despair.

"Fuck, look." We all jump at the sound of Steven's voice. He points his long arm and we follow his gaze. People are coming with wood, with tools and music tech. Punks … goths … indie kids … Our fucking listeners are here. They are here to fucking save Riot Radio.

Just in case you were wondering how our beloved listeners were able to pull this off….. They banded together and got permits from the city. Apparently a bunch of indie kids and punks demanding to put their favourite radio station back together are very convincing.

Anyways back to our happy ending.

Day in and day out we feed them and in return they help lift beams, nail wood and put walls back together. They even helped to set up the control centre. They give us their old and rare records and the indie kids bring in new stuff they want us to play. Every fucking day I don't expect them to come back. Every fucking day they are here.

In a matter of weeks we stand in a finished Riot Radio station, cheering, with cans of beer and heaps of greasy food. I'm sitting on a speaker, dangling my legs. Ben is kissing Taylor softly. Cassandra has her arm around a gorgeous trans girl and Timothy is smiling with his arms around David's shoulders.

The door opens and the band *New Americana* comes in. The lead singer struts in with tight black leather pants and a black leather jacket. She looks up at me and breaks out into a grin. I grin back.

Ben—he's never left my side. He's still the manager who keeps me happy and sane. He is still happily dating Taylor.

Taylor—he got his top surgery and is still working at Riot Radio. He is still happily dating Ben.

Cassandra—is helping me host LGBTQ talks and debates. She is still our savvy tech girl. She is dating a gorgeous trans girl named Rose.

As for me, I don't threaten listeners anymore ... well not as much. My mental health is still a struggle, but Riot Radio and my family there keeps me together. In case you haven't guessed it yet, I'm dating, Lauren, the lead singer from *New Americana*.

To all the punk rock, goth and indie kids out there—never stop being you. Celebrate your inner freak and fight back in whatever ever way you can to change this world.

Sasha Miller Forever a punk rock kid!